GRIM WORK

JON HILLMAN

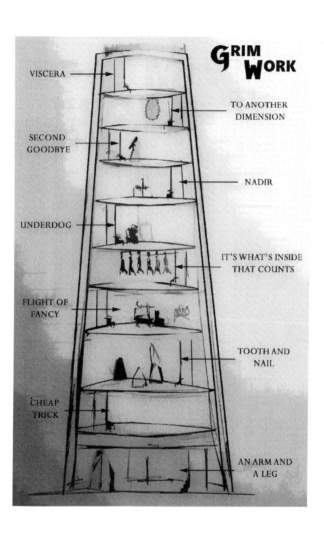

GRIM WORK

Chapter One

AN ARM AND A LEG

Marigold stormed inside the tower. He booted shut the great wooden doors that swung behind him. "Fucking wizards," he seethed through his clenched teeth.

The darkness within the vaulted ceilings of the tower's ground floor crept over Marigold, and the last of the daylight was snuffed out by the closing entrance. A hollow thud filled the cavernous floor, drowning out the last of the pained cries from the soldiers left outside. The bird could handle the rest of it alone; she was more than a match for that pathetic excuse of a guard.

"Fucking wizards," he repeated, spitting onto flagstones that were soft with green moss. "Rat-hearted fucking wizards and their pissing, Pit-cursed spires." He raised his head and bellowed into the darkness, "Do your gods demand you live in these shitty hovels? You enjoy climbing up and down this each day?"

No response.

Marigold grunted like some feral beast. He hefted the limp body he had slung over his broad shoulders to a more comfortable position. Marigold was strong – he was very strong – but a deadweight was a deadweight no matter which way you looked at it. "Can't just live in a bloody tent or shack like normal folk. Can't make this easy, can you? Prick. Just dragging out the inevitable."

It wasn't the first time that Marigold had entered such a construction with a burning desire to rid the world of one more magical bastard, and it most certainly would not be the last. These, however, a set of circumstances that he had no desire to see a repeat of.

Marigold: A husband without a wife. Marigold: a friend without friends. Marigold: a chief without a clan. All of these things threatened to crush him where he stood, but now that he was in the tower of 'Cezare the Perpetrator' there was no longer any time for breaking down over it. Time to focus on what was to come. Cezare. Just Cezare. Time to start a new life, right here, right now. This tower and its goat-shagging mage were going to witness Marigold's glorious rebirth, and it was going to be fucking bloody.

Marigold's hulking, muscular frame swaggered into the middle of the dim space. A remarkably plain room, just like the exterior. Narrow pillars reached floor to ceiling, and a staircase was built into a squared column at the far end of the hall. It was a big entrance. Well, it was a huge tower. The sconces hanging from the curved walls were all unlit, every one of them. Good that there was barely anything to fucking see in the first place. No movement came from the recesses. No surprise attacks from cloaked assassins. No more clusters of young soldiers not yet ready to meet their ends in their first fight. Most importantly, there was no shitting spellcaster. Nothing. He was all alone in the foyer. It really was fucking disappointing; it wasn't as though he was paying the prick a surprise visit.

Marigold dumped the body from his shoulder onto the hard flagstones. The heavy thud of slack flesh echoed like a drum about the dark space. A small cloud of dirt and grit floated up from below and settled upon the wretch. Some doorman he had been. The coward had put his hands up in front of his face instead of fighting back. Naturally, Marigold had split that fucking face in two. Poor bastard had probably died of fright before the fist even connected.

The shouting outside picked up. It was definitely closer.

"Do your fucking job, bird," Marigold growled. He refused to call it Sofia. Her previous owner, Sieg, had been the one to name her, not he. Sieg was dead now. Marigold was simply borrowing her, and just needed her to do as she was told. Rukhs themselves were fine mounts, and fierce as the worst of the devils from the Pit, but their intelligence was somewhat lacking. Perhaps Marigold had been too trusting to think that the beast would finish the remainder of the job he had left outside.

The tower doors might have been shut, but they weren't locked.

"Shit. That won't bloody do, now, will it?" he muttered. He did not need somebody creeping up behind him and shoving a knife into his back while he was about his tasks in here.

Each door had a heavy, brass handle. A metal loop that he could slide a plank through for a makeshift barricade. Wouldn't last long, but might give him enough time to head up a floor or two. If he was right – and he usually was – this tower was going to be laden with bloody traps from bottom to top. If anybody else made it inside, they weren't going to chase him far. Wizards loved a fucking funhouse, and Marigold very much doubted that this cunt would be any different. Must be nice to have the time to think up all of the elaborate nonsense that he was about to put himself through.

Anyway, whatever he was about to face, Marigold didn't have a bloody plank.

He pawed at his claymore, Sear, strapped to his back. It would be a crying shame to part with her before she got to slice or burn anything. He pulled her from his back and held her in both arms. His grey eyes reflected back at him from the polished centre of the blade. Eyes that had seen too much. Weary eyes. He couldn't leave her down here. Where would his catharsis come from if he gave her up now? Tearing things apart with fingers and teeth was great, but shoving thick, ragged metal into a foe and watching it rend the flesh and spill the blood as it was slowly pulled out was what he really wanted to get out of this. No, his sword was not going to barricade any fucking door, by Greldin's celestial axe, that cut of steel death was sticking firmly to his back for the main event. He slid her back into her sheath. Tearing things apart, though? Now there was a thought.

Marigold eyed the body on the floor.

Bodies had several plank-like appendages, and this one wasn't likely to need any of them ever again.

Marigold grasped a floppy wrist between his palms and wedged his thick, hide boot beneath the shoulder. He pulled. Muscles knotted, wrapping around one another like snakes writhing beneath his skin. The guard's arm stretched, the bones inside ground together noisily. A wet tearing sound was followed shortly by a hollow pop. Years ago, when Marigold had first ripped a man's arm from his body, he thought that he would never want to hear that sound again. It turned out it would become one of the more frequent sounds he would end up hearing over the years. It turned out that it *was* something you could get used to.

Marigold presented the severed limb to the closed doors. He stretched it out and slotted it in behind the burnished metal handles. It fit snugly. The dead fellow might not have put up anything resembling a fight, but credit where credit was due, he had some impressive biceps. "Hmm." He pulled at the top of the handle. There was still a lot of movement in the elbow. The kind of movement that would see the bastard thing give up just as easily as its owner had. More limbs were needed. A femur ought to do the job quite well.

Marigold turned back to face the body in the middle of the room and stopped dead. Its fucking eyes were wide open, and clearly in a state of utter shock. From what Marigold could see beneath the strings of snot and blood, the man appeared to be gasping quite heavily.

"Sorry friend," Marigold offered, crouching down on his haunches by the fellow, "for what it's worth, I thought you were dead. Really, I did." He shuffled around to the man's head and wrapped his arms around his neck. Now he could feel a pulse. Typical. "You're obviously stronger than you look. Or act."

"Wh-wh-wha… What… wh…"

"Hmm? What? Spit it out, for fuck's sake."

"Wh-what…" the man gasped, "are you… d-doing?"

"What do you think I'm doing? I can't fucking leave you like this, can I? I'm a barbarian, not a bastard."

"B-b-but you… y-y-you j-just apo-po-po-logised!" The man began to leak out pathetic sobs.

By Greldin. A true coward. Just what had happened to all of the good warriors these days? "You're right, I did apologise. For the undue suffering I've just gone and put you through. Doesn't change what has to come next. One way or another, you're dying in here, and you're dying today."

"L-l-leave me to die, then!" he shrieked.

"Friend," Marigold sighed. He really didn't have time for this pissing about. Every moment wasted meant another breath that would fill the wizard's lungs. "I've nothing against you, but my opinion on whether or not you should be dead or alive right now is no different than it was when I first lugged you in through that door. Now, I need one of those legs of yours, and I'm sure you'd rather not be around to feel that being pulled off too."

"N-n-no! No! Y-you can't! You can't do this!" The man's whimpering and shaking was doing something rotten to his insides, blood gushed forth from his mouth, pooling in the dust below.

"I can," Marigold confirmed. "And you can rest assured that I'll do it right this time. Fuck's sake, you couldn't make this shit up."

"I-I've a, a, a f-family."

"And you'll fucking still have one whether you're here for them or not. I'm killing you, not them!" Marigold said, baffled. What in the world was wrong with the wimp?

The man began to weep uncontrollably.

"Look, I'll give you a choice."

The man's eyes lit up, despite his grievous – and fatal – circumstances.

"I'll just leave you here and-" Marigold gripped tightly and twisted, hard. The snap came almost instantaneously. A momentary look of horror crossed the man's eyes before his eyelids drooped and his pupils slid off in opposing directions. A final, wheezing breath whispered out, and only then did Marigold realise just how tightly the bastard had been digging in with his remaining hand. Prick had left some deep nail marks decorating his forearm. That was one for the stories, if he ever had a clan to tell them to again.

It took a couple of yanks to separate leg from hip. The release of pressure sent a spurt of blood up Marigold's side, soaking into the hairs of his animal skin jerkin. It wasn't the first blood that had soaked him this day, and it most certainly wouldn't be the last. He expected to be bathed in the fucking stuff before he was done in here.

The addition of the leg did the job, as expected. He placed the knee facing the door. In the end it would snap inwards, but it would take a few heaves. Despite his hard work, it had gone somewhat quiet outside. That rukh was a selfish bitch of a bird, but Marigold did hope that she wasn't lying in a broken heap of blood, feathers, and beak. He was going to need a ride home after this was done and dusted.

Marigold returned to the body and kicked it heavily in the ribs, half expecting those eyes to be glaring at him once again. "Hope your ghost can come to understand what needed to be done here," he told it. "You're doing a far grander job of keeping fuckers out now than you did while you were whole, though. I've done you a bloody favour."

Satisfied that the door was in a decent enough state to leave now, Marigold paced through the gloom of the ground floor to the base of the upwards stairs. How many floors did this fucker have, then? Five? Ten? Twenty? These goat-fondling, spell-casting pricks just loved to look down on people. It was bizarre. And they never, ever placed their amenities on the lower floors. Kept everything useful to them right at the bastard top. To be perfectly honest, Marigold had no idea how often these cunts even left their towers — maybe they could simply summon everything they needed without ever having to leave — but it had to be a real pain in the ringpiece when you actually had to come down. He'd never met this Cezare, but the shithead must have some impressive legs on him.

Marigold found himself stroking his long, dirty-blonde beard as he considered what lay above. "Won't do to have some girl grab it in the middle of scrap, will it?" he mumbled to himself. Marigold plucked a small but sharp knife from his boot. He began to hack at his beard. It wasn't a close shave by any stretch of the imagination, but it was a finger and thumb job if anybody was going to get a hold of it. He did the same for the hair that hung in a short ponytail down his back. He probably looked an absolute state, but who gave a shit? There was no time to look pretty in a fight anyway, and Marigold was far from pretty in the first place.

Taking on a tower alone. Fucking moons-crazed fool. He'd done it before, but that was some years ago now. He wasn't young anymore, but he was wiser. Probably stronger too. Shit, this was probably going to go better than ever. Still, he would have preferred to have Vik or Sieg or Haggar – or any of the others – along for the ride. Might be that they were watching over him from Greldin's halls, but that was no use in a scrap.

Marigold got to thinking about Cezare again. What kind of magic-dabbler was he? There were so many to keep track of. Magicians had more magic in their title than anything else, and were little more than rogues that used sleight-of-hand to dazzle people into losing their purses. Marigold wouldn't be here if Cezare was one of those. He wasn't stood in a forest, so it wasn't a Druid up top. He had easily found the tower, so he was unlikely to be facing an Illusionist. Alchemists weren't particularly violent. It was unfortunate, but judging by the bastard's grand diversion and the state of Marigold's camp, the sack of shit was more than likely a Conjuror, a Summoner, or a Necromancer. Maybe a shitty combination of all three. A halfwit that thought fiddling with the unseen planes was a fine idea. Contracts and demons and death. Fucking perfect.

Whatever discipline this prick followed, retribution would find him just the same.

"So, Cezare," he bellowed into the stairwell, kicking the pile of cut hair from around his feet. "What fucking entertainment do you have waiting for me up there, then?"

The steps melted into the darkness. Fitting for what was about to come. Marigold felt the chill of Death, waiting eagerly on his shoulder. But Death was not waiting for Marigold's soul. No, Death was along for the fun of it all, to revel in the glorious flow of blood, the screams of agony, the collection of souls. Death's scythe grew rusty while it accompanied Marigold. After all, why would Death need a weapon of its own when it had Marigold's blade and hands and teeth to do the work?

Chapter Two

CHEAP TRICK

The staircase spun round and round. Not exactly wide enough to have a scrap in, should the worst come to pass. Always best to get out of tight spaces while you still could. Marigold leapt up the steps as a slight confusion took him; that floor below had a high ceiling, but it hadn't been *that* high.

Marigold's heart pounded. Not with the exertion of bounding upwards. Not with the fear of any encounter. It pounded with pure excitement. Anticipation! All things considered, Marigold was going through a rough time. Some of the roughest times he had ever known in his forty-odd winters. He didn't lose a clan every day, didn't have to bury people every day. He never wanted to have to bury someone so close to him again, and he didn't want to have to think about the wife he would never hold again. But it had happened. It was done. Marigold had always found that a good fight dealt with grief most agreeably, and he was very eager for the comfort that this tower was going to offer. Smashing teeth, crushing necks, bursting eyes… It was all such a fucking rush. And the screams his enemies cried out! Music to the ears. Vindication. Only the guilty screamed. That's how you knew you had the right one. A proud man met his death with grim determination and silence; another hurdle that one's spirit inevitably had to leap over at some point, be it through old age or a blade to the heart. A guilty man raged. A guilty man wept at the sheer injustice of being denied further breath. After all, what was the point in doing evil if it wasn't going to extend your life? Well, perhaps that was how they thought. Or maybe they didn't see their own doings as evil. Marigold wasn't completely sure; he wasn't that type of person. But whatever the truth really was, Marigold's observations of his victims thus far seemed to indicate that it was a sense of unfairness that they felt in their last moments.

The warrior erupted out from the rising passage and into the open of the next floor. And this one really *was* open.

"Fuck me," Marigold groaned. Floor two was even emptier than the first. There weren't any pillars on this one, nor was there a mangled corpse decorating the stones underfoot. Pity. The place could do with a little sprucing up. Like below, there were no windows slit into the walls here either. The only light was a single burning torch on the far side of the level, an all too obvious indicator of where Cezare intended Marigold to go. Trap one approached. The warm up. But what was it? Marigold studied what he could in the murk. He pawed at the rounded pommel of Sear, as she rested behind his head. His thick fingers caressed her hilt, lifting her hefty frame and dropping her back down. Marigold liked a fight. He didn't like surprises. There was bound to be something going on in here. The fucking wizard wasn't just going to let him just stroll up and hack the head from his shoulders, was he? At least he really hoped that wasn't going to be the case. "Come on! What is it you're hiding, prick?"

"Welcome, Marigold." A slimy and self-satisfied voice came from everywhere at once. It filled the huge room.

"Finally," Marigold laughed, "the soon-to-be-dead cunt makes an appearance with the cheapest of tricks. If you thought that would make me shit myself you'll be sorely disappointed." He waved a hand over his arse. "Dry," he mocked. Marigold swaggered onwards, pushing into the dismal hall. "Honestly, I've lost count of the number times some wand-waving spell-fumbler tried that one on me. Each and every one of them soon found themselves with light shoulders."

"Charming, my friend. I did hear that you had quite the way with words. I'm so pleased to finally hear you for myself. Tell me, are you all talk, or is there something more to you?"

Marigold ground his teeth and snarled. Self-absorbed fucking abscess of a man. Stoneless bastard sounded young too. Far too cocky for someone of such an age, although it wouldn't be the first time he'd found a magic-user capable of making himself appear younger. "Expected thanks for all you've done for me? A warm greeting? A slap on the fucking back?"

"Well, I-"

"Y'can still hope. See, when we stand face-to-face – and we will be doing so – there'll be warmth. Oh, you can fucking bet on it. Just a shame for you that it'll be red and wet, and yours."

"Maybe you'll get that meeting sooner than you think," the voice snapped.

A crackling tore the air, sparks flew and the space before Marigold seemed to congeal into a misty, white shape. From within the mass came the figure of a black-robed man, face hidden within a darkened cowl. Strings of lank, black hair hung out from each side. Projection. Men didn't just appear out of nowhere otherwise.

"You think that's going to impress me? I've fucking seen that too." Marigold wrenched Sear from his back and thrust her into the spell, just in case. It dissipated into nothing, as was largely expected.

The voice tutted angrily from everywhere in the room. Unintelligible grumbles.

"Maybe you should think about working on the tricks you show your guests?" Marigold grunted. "Didn't realise I was taking on the court-fucking-jester."

"Well, well, well. I can see now that you're a very learned barbarian, Marigold. My mistake. But, while I'm sure your muscles and wit have served you well in the past, we'll see how that delicious organ you call a brain copes with the rest of my tower." The voice began to cackle. The kind of cackle that only someone with considerable delusions of grandeur would ever dare let slip. The kind of screech that implied madness and got you hanged in a heartbeat in the city. "I think you'll come to appreciate my work very much, Marigold."

"When it results in you being dead, then yes, I really fucking will."

Silence.

Marigold didn't call out again. Prick had ended his spell. The Pit-bound cunt was probably heaving and groaning on the floor of his study after wearing himse-

A white, clawed hand burst out of thin air. Long, outstretched fingers flexed as they hurtled towards Marigold.

With barely a moment to think about it, Marigold felt icy fingers wrap themselves around his throat. "Fucking what?" This *was* something new. Something unexpected. The fingers tightened, the claw tips dug into his jugular. Marigold grappled at the constricting digits, his free hand passing through the apparition. He began pawing at his own bloody neck instead. "Fugghin… wiz… ardsss!" There was no panic yet. It wasn't the first time his enemies had thought that air was the only thing keeping him going, and it wouldn't be the last. Over the years, he had built up an impressive ability to hold it. He had a good few minutes before he was in any real trouble.

Still, a few minutes were no good if he just spent them choking to death.

Think.

Think!

Marigold had very little to consider with his plain surroundings. The only movement apart from his twisting and turning was the flickering torch at the end of the room. The first flames of the tower. There was as much chance of that being coincidence as anything else, but they needed to be put out.

Cezare's laughing returned. The walls seemed to bend inwards with the noise. All part of the spell. Even this caster wouldn't be stupid enough to bring his own tower down around him.

The grip tightened. Marigold staunched his desire to spout insults, contenting himself to reel each one off in his head. He lurched towards the torch and staircase. Halfway.

Either he was being dragged further away or the torch was sliding out of reach. The effect made Marigold quite nauseous, but he refused to show it. Shit, it was difficult to show much of anything at this point anyway. Sear fell from his grip. Metal struck stone and rang out around the hall. Marigold's ears throbbed.

Just barely did he register the sinking and scraping of the stone slab beneath his leaden feet.

Marigold instinctively fell backwards as a metallic slice drew upwards into the room. Rows of thin, spear-tipped poles burst forth from the floor below and the ceiling above. As the pieces of the trap hissed past each other, dividing the floor into two halves, Marigold hit the flagstones, shoulder blades first. The blow beat the remaining gasps of air from his lungs.

The gripping hand vanished into nothingness, and Marigold found his own fingers tightening around his neck in their search for it.

Sweet, sweet air filled Marigold's lungs. He sucked at it eagerly. His fingers regained their strength.

"Prick!" he yelled.

Marigold spent a couple of moments lying on his back, massaging his neck and coughing. That was one for the fucker in the robe. A new trick. He hadn't seen that before, and he hated surprises. How in the Pits had he rid himself of the shitting thing, anyway? Fell over? Didn't seem right. Had the ghostly fingers even been there in there in the first place? It had hurt – not much, just a tingle – but he couldn't find any cuts or wounds where it had gripped, no bruises under the skin, no blood. Nothing at all. Fucking magic.

The cunt was testing him.

For whatever reason, Cezare seemed to *want* Marigold to climb further up into his house of tricks. The mystic imbecile had a death wish, but it was with a sense of trepidation that Marigold found himself grabbing Sear and using her to haul himself back up. He rarely felt that, and he wasn't bloody happy about it.

The spear barrier stretched from one side of the circular room to the other. No wonder he had climbed a lot of steps to this floor, there had to be at least twice his height in stone beneath him to house all of this fucking metal. Same above. What kind of madman designed a tower like this? It wasn't something you could just shove in on a whim, this had to be part of the original plan.

Marigold decided that the only thing he was ever going to understand about these spell-spouting bungholes was that they died just like anybody else when a blade was pushed inside them. The sooner that occurred with this one, the better.

Marigold seized one of the slender spears that still trembled before him. He jerked it towards himself and snapped it clean from its repository; so small that that it was no wonder he missed it in the shadows. He studied the tip; sharp, to be sure, but the metal it was attached to was so thin that it seemed that it would bend or snap instead of pierce its intended target. He cast the length of metal to the stones, where it bounced with a tinny rattle. "Fucking pathetic. Waste of time."

Nevertheless, Marigold found himself staring at each remaining stone before he stepped on it, lest another wave of lances be buried somewhere beneath him. "I must look a complete piss weasel, hopping this way and that," he grumbled. "I hope you're enjoying the fucking show, Cezare."

No answer.

Who knew whether Cezare was really able to watch? Could he just project his voice? Marigold didn't really care. Let the Deadman laugh, it was the last enjoyment he would have.

After his slow creep across the room, the mighty warrior found himself at the foot of the next rise of curling steps. His shadow flickered beneath the flame of the torch. Out of little more than spite for it, Marigold plucked the burning wood from its metal loop and cast it to the floor. The room became entirely dark as he crushed the glowing embers beneath his foot. He spat in disgust and entered the pillar of stairs.

Marigold's boot missed the first step.

His foot disappeared from beneath him. His shin struck the sharp edge of the next step. Agony shot through his leg. Up, up, up it went, settling deep within his stones. It wasn't the first time he'd made a tit out of himself, and it would most certainly not be the last, but at least he always managed to weather accidents like this out of the sight of anybody else. The darkness here was a gift, even if it was his own doing as well as the cause. "You fucking missed that one!" he laughed. "First blood your shitty tower's had out of me."

THE CONTRACT

Marigold sat on his wooden seat at the back of his goatskin yurt. He watched yet another farmer leave. Five so far today, and there were at least another five yet to come that he was aware of. He yawned loudly and shifted in his chair. Funny how the most tiring work of all was the work that required him to remain seated on his arse all day, sun up to sun down.

There had been a common theme of the day thus far. Goats. Or rather, a marked lack of the horned, devil-eyed bastards. High up in the rocky and grassy hills of Illis, South Rosaria, goats were the livestock of choice. They didn't tend to fall from the cliffs as much as sheep, or rukhs, or horses. Sure-footed little rascals, they were. Could usually forget about them and still find you had the bulk of them alive when you needed meat, milk, leather, or drinking horns. When a man couldn't make himself a new drinking horn… well, that was when shit started to get heated. The only thing goats weren't any good for was wood, stone and steel. The surrounding hills had that in abundance anyway. Marigold hadn't yet worked out where the goats had been disappearing to, but each and every one of his visitors today had sworn that Cezare, a sorcerer that dwelt in a tower not too far from the current site of Marigold's clan, was the man responsible. But, a lot of goats had gone missing. A huge number. Enough that you'd probably notice if one person had them, especially one so nearby. The farmers demanded blood, but Marigold liked to think these matters through a little more than that. He relished a fight as much as the next brute, but there was always more to consider when it came to tackling some magical prick. How powerful were they? What magic did they dabble in? Had the fucker actually done it? Marigold had spent a good number of years before settling in this land travelling with his lads, rooting out those wand-waving arseholes, and putting them in the ground. Or throwing them from a tower. Or feeding them to some animal. He'd garnered quite the reputation for it, and the dead hadn't always been guilty. Those that studied magics tended to avoid him now, and there was no reason to believe that this... Cezare, was any different to them. And whether the man was guilty or not, since finding his wife and settling into life, Marigold had found his desire to kill wizards somewhat diminished.

"Next," he called lazily, shifting his numb arse on the frame of his chair once again.

Elvi appeared. Raven-haired, beautiful and fierce. Marigold's woman. She ushered in a little man with a weasel-like face. The fellow was dressed in a purple doublet with gold details around the shoulders. Black breeches and expensive-looking leather boots completed the look; the kind you would only ever see worn by folk from the city. Clothes that were useless out here in the wilds. A pendulous necklace swung from his neck. Clearly gold, and clearly intended as a display of wealth. The little shit wouldn't last five minutes out on his own; he had to have some grand entourage waiting outside for him. As Elvi brought the odious little fellow closer, she gave a wry smile to her husband. Marigold caught her scent, let his tongue taste her. He gave himself a moment to admire her figure, openly desiring her before the crowd. She looked him up and down in return. He turned to his visitor and opened his palms. Marigold watched the visitor's eyes darting back and forth around the bright yurt, taking everything in, and looking vaguely disgusted with what he saw.

"A Mr. Dahl has travelled to meet us, husband." Elvi patted the man's back and nudged him toward Marigold. She tossed her thick, black hair about and gathered it between her hands behind her neck. She really was a welcome distraction on days like this.

"Thank you, Elvi." He lazily waved a hand and Elvi retreated to a seat at the edge of the yurt, alongside Marigold's huge friends Sieg, Magnus, and Haggar. Marigold watched her sit, then nodded lightly at the rows of solemn clan members that always sat in on such meetings. Finally, he settled on his new visitor. "Don't recognise you, friend. Not from around here, are you?"

"Oh no, Lord Marigold, not from around here at all. I've travelled from the east, between the mountains, from a city you may know? Hvitstein, The White City. Speaks volumes for how far I have had to travel to find a man that would be capable of removing my, er, my little problem."

"Spit it out then," he asked as nicely as he could. "I've plenty more folk waiting to see me, and I don't have all day to skirt around the specifics of your 'little problem' while there are still goats going missing out there."

"Of course, well, I say little, it's err, ha, a-a *little*, ha, more than that. So to speak."

Marigold sighed. Fucking city-folk. They were never straightforward. They always wanted everything to sound more complex than it was, more detailed and important than anything else that could ever happen outside their own lives. It was going to have to be something bloody impressive indeed to interest him now.

"We've a gargunnoch problem."

Oh. That caused Marigold to sit up. "Gargunnochs, you say?"

"Well, just the one to be precise, but the most enormous specimen that you ever did see," Dahl regaled his small crowd, obviously pleased that the big, hairy, muscle-bound men were now leaning in with obvious interest. "And not only is it a veritable titan, it's white too. Did you ever see a white gargunnoch, Lord Marigold?"

"No. And it all sounds very impressive, but right now I'm only feeling like you want me to pat you on the head for simply knowing about it. What's it done that has brought you all the way out here?"

"Terrible things, my lord!"

Here we go. Marigold slunk back into his chair, rested his elbow on the arm and his chin on his palm.

"The white gargunnoch brings terror and destruction to our fair walls. Farmers can't farm, men can't ride their rukhs about, children cannot play outside."

"A fucking disaster," Marigold deadpanned.

"Indeed," Dahl nodded vehemently.

"Has it killed anybody?"

"Beg your pardon?"

"Dead. Who is dead? Chomped, trampled, gored by the beast. Is this white gargunnoch of the White City a terror, or is it just a nuisance?"

"Oh, it is most definitely the former, Lord Marigold. Most definitely." The weasel began wringing his hands together, eyes continually darting this way and that. Shifty bastard, though he was probably just terrified to be surrounded by real men and women.

"Fine, so it needs to be killed. What do you think? I can send three, or four of my men?"

"Oh, but Lord Marigold. I have travelled in the shadow of the white gargunnoch. I have fled through plains, over mountains, between the great trees of the forests to reach you. I have come here specifically because my master has requested that you, directly, come to take care of the beast."

Marigold slapped his wide palm over his face. He pinched his eyebrows together and exhaled into his hand. "Me? I've plenty of business here already. I can't just-"

"Tales of your deeds are known throughout the land, Lord Marigold. Beasts you have slain, rogues you have torn asunder, bandits that no longer cut a purse. Everyone has heard the stories of you and your... your..." he pointed to the huge claymore that lay resting by Marigold's seat.

"Sear."

"Mmm... Let me cut right to it then. The payment will be excellent, I assure you. I-I assure you *all*." He performed a slow spin around the yurt, acknowledging everyone as he held his arms open wide.

Olaf, a younger warrior with a lot to learn about subtlety, stepped towards Dahl. "Gold is useless to us, little one," he barked. "Got all we need of that with our chief right there, ain't that right, boss?"

By Greldin's celestial fucking axe! Marigold tried to keep the disdain from his face. His boys all loved that their chief had a sharp tongue. They all wanted to be just like him in that regard. Well, not Haggar, but then he had no tongue. Marigold was sure that Olaf thought his gold comment was very clever, but even calm Elvi was trying her hardest to bite her tongue. Right now, it was best just to let him believe that it was clever, but the Pits knew that his dead ancestors were probably laughing their ghostly fucking boots off after hearing that.

"Of course, of course!" Dahl simpered. "We wouldn't insult barb- er, hah, warriors with such a display."

"Barbarians?" Marigold snapped. "Fucking barbarians. That's all we are to you, isn't it? Savages in tents that eat their food alive, fuck animals, and live for nothing but killing." Marigold stepped up from his chair, collecting Sear from his side. He began to pace a slow circle around Dahl. Now that he stood, he found he was almost twice the size of the shit. "Just get the cunts with the swords to do the dirty work. Doesn't matter which of them live or die, that's of no concern to the man in the city."

"I..." Dahl began to tremble in the shadow of the enormous clan leader.

"What is it that makes you look down on us?" He tapped the tip of Sear on the frightened man's shoulder. "Metaphorically speaking, of course."

"Please, Lord Mari-"

"Is it because... *we don't shpeak sho good*?" he mocked, shaking his long and fair hair from side to side. "Because we live in tents instead of laid stone? Because we have no need for gold? Gold doesn't make blades, my friend." For good measure, the clan chief began flexing his arms as he paced, swinging Sear this way and that. His bulging muscles tightened, catching the light in the yurt. Murmurings picked up from both sides of the room. Elvi clasped her hands together, Sieg mumbled in agreement with his chief. Near the exit, black-haired and topless Vik planted his hands on his hips, nodding and grinning menacingly at the guest. Mute Haggar smiled viciously. Marigold finally stopped in front of the man. He crouched, leaning on his sword so that his eyes were level with the wildly perspiring Dahl. In a stroke of unplanned luck, the yurt darkened as the clouds outside covered the sun. Marigold's face was bathed in shadow. "What's the payment?" he demanded.

"W-w-w-we have food, livestock, land. All of these things could be-"

"What livestock?"

"Rukhs, goats, chickens."

"Goats."

"Err, my lord?"

"How many goats?"

"We could offer... five hundred?"

"Double it."

"My lord," Dahl began to laugh nervously, "that would be almost all of goats we have. Surely some grain, or-or... Or wood? Metal? Iron?"

"You came through woodland to get here. There are caves riddling these hills, bursting at their seams with the metals we need. What we're missing are goats, and we'll take no fewer than one thousand for a gargunnoch. But don't worry, we won't ask for any more. We're fair people."

"I-I-I can s-see that, believe me."

A pregnant silence descended among the inhabitants of the tent. It quickly became uncomfortable. Men shifted from foot to foot, sighs leaked out, Dahl's swallowing sounded like it was taking place outside his own throat.

"Very well," Dahl agreed, breaking the silence. He began to pull a rolled-up parchment from his doublet. "Do you have a quill about?"

"We're barbarians, remember?" Marigold slipped his dagger from a strap on his ankle. He flicked the point into the tip of his thumb and rubbed his forefinger over the fresh slit to smear the blood. Some folk enjoyed the drama of dragging the blade across their palm, but not Marigold. It was all very good from a showman's perspective, but it was no use if you were going to need to swing your sword any time soon after. He snatched the paper from Dahl and pressed his thumb onto the bottom of it. "That do for your fucking signature?"

"Perfect, my lord," he grinned, rolling the sheet back up. "I'll get this back to my master."

"Haggar," Marigold called, "escort Mr. Dahl back out to his people."

"Oh, my lord," Dahl chimed in, "I travelled here alone."

"Did you really?" Marigold narrowed his eyes at the back of the man as silent Haggar pulled the skin over the door aside and ushered the man out. "Fucking city folk," he murmured after him.

The remaining petitioners of the day were all local. All local, and *all* bemoaning their missing livestock. Marigold managed to temporarily sate them all with the news of the thousand incoming goats, but he was going to have to tackle the heart of the matter soon, especially if the next batch of livestock met a similar fate.

"So, my favourite barbarian," Elvi sat on Marigold's knee and draped her pale arms around her husband's sturdy neck as the yurt began to clear. "A white gargunnoch! Are you excited?"

"Well," he began, kissing the side of her neck below the ear, "these missing goats have been troubling me more, to tell the truth. Where is a man to find his fun when his beloved goat is missing?"

"That is a worry, husband of mine. You could ask one of your friends, though I may have a solution to hand."

The sun had left the skies long before Marigold and Elvi lay still for the night. A tangle of gold and black hair covered him, and he felt a sense of peace that was strange for a man such as he to feel, though he wasn't averse to it. A life of hard work, battles, and loss had brought him to this point. He had earned this ease. Marigold lay with his hands behind his head, drinking in the quiet breathing of his sleeping wife. He *was* excited. It had been months since the last hunt, and that had only been for deer. A gargunnoch was something big. Something huge. It was a fucking monster, the kind of thing he had spent so much of his youth hunting. Ease was all well and good, but a fight now and then didn't go amiss, and he didn't want Sear to rust. Sleep just wouldn't come. He found himself watching the eastern edge of the tent for the first light, the signal to go.

There it was.

"Vik!" he bellowed.

"Chief?" came a reply from the closest tent.

"Saddle up Gretel, and the other rukhs. Shaggy bitches haven't had a good run in ages, and we're off to Hvitstein."

Chapter Three

TOOTH AND NAIL

At last, a floor with a little more character than the dingy spaces below. The third of the rising circles spread out before Marigold, lit up by the first windows of the tower. Shafts of light poured through, illuminating three stone domes set on the tiles, and an array of chains that reached from them up to the ceiling. They were situated just so that the light happened to catch each of them right now. Another coincidence, or did Cezare control the sun as well? He couldn't have planned that little scuffle downstairs so well that Marigold was always destined to find these stones lit just as they were? Spellcasters made Marigold think too much. Made his skin fucking crawl. You always had to factor in more than face value when fighting magic. Fucking wizards.

The steps for the next floor were, once again, directly ahead. Closer, as the tower began to taper upwards, but this particular exit was blocked with iron bars and chains and a great, fuck-off lock right in the centre. A puzzle. Surely the bookworm knew that Marigold's type weren't really the thoughtful kind? Whatever. It had to be something to do with the domes.

"I give up, Cezare. You win. What do I do?"

No response.

"I did so enjoy our conversation, you cock-rotted rukh shit…"

Minutes passed with no word. The gleam was starting to slide from the domes onto the light-grey flagstones around them.

"Suppose I'll have to work it out for myself then." Marigold paced around the domes, running his hands along the smoothed stone and metal straps with rusted rivets. He rapped his knuckles across one and received a hollow boom in response. Thin. The other domes responded in kind. Dull grunts began to pick up. "I do enjoy gifts. Just tell me, what is it?" He stood before the locked door, gripping the bars that blocked the way. "By Greldin!" he growled. To the Pits with the puzzle, he just needed to get upstairs. In growing frustration, he jabbed the tip of his knife into the lock. A grinding began to shake within the ceiling above. The chains that had dangled freely became taught and began retracting into some sort of machinery between the floors.

Finally.

Marigold slid his knife back into his boot and watched eagerly as the lifting domes revealed clawed feet. Three toes. Grey, warty skin. Up the domes went. Thick legs, a distinct lack of genitalia. Sharp-nailed fingers wriggled out from underneath the dome, trying to speed up the process. Feet stamped, grunts and snorts grew louder. Marigold drew Sear from his back, clutching her hilt tightly in two hands. His heart pounded. A physical fight was finally on the cusp of kicking off. None of that intangible shit from the floor below. He smiled as the domes reached the ceiling, revealing the misshapen heads, yellow eyes, and toothy maws of his foes.

Skags.

Three of the hunch-backed bastards. Common inhabitants of mountain caves and dark forests, not fucking towers.

They snorted and puffed out their enormous chests, then charged straight towards him in silence, arms outstretched.

Marigold wasted no time. He swung Sear in a wide arc through the space between himself and his foes. She sung as she sliced the air, ceasing her melody only for a moment as she cut deep into the eyes of the creature closest. The victim stumbled back, clutching its face as yellow fluid leaked between thick fingers. The first ragged bellow filled the room.

"On you come," Marigold taunted, clapping at the hilt of his blade. He reckoned he had two or three minutes before that first one would wade back into the fight. Skags had the irritating ability to regenerate their flesh. Made them difficult foes. Ideally, you would fight them one at a time, but that didn't look to be a luxury available to Marigold today.

Marigold was thrown backwards as the second one to arrive grappled his shoulders. Even with the barbarian's obscene strength, he couldn't bring Sear back into the fray like that. She clattered to the floor as the impact threw his palms open. That itself was nothing to worry about, a skag wouldn't use a tool. Marigold bent to try and throw the bastard from him. No use. He almost kicked himself in the stones as he brought his boot up to get his dagger into reach. Out came the small blade, and into the skag's neck it plunged, rammed deep as number three came to take over. The skag Marigold now named 'Neck' gurgled sickeningly as it was let go with the weapon still wedged inside. The barbarian threw his massive fist at Three's face. It wobbled slightly, shook its head. Concussion was likely too much to hope for with these brainless shits. Three surged forward and smashed its rough shoulder into Marigold's chest. Marigold grunted like the beasts he was fighting. He stumbled back, determined not to topple. It was some fucking monster that could throw him off balance like that. He tensed his mighty legs, recovered, and readied himself for the next blow that had already been launched.

Only it breezed by, inches from his face.

Marigold felt pressure on his shoulders. Felt himself being spun around.

Yellow eyes with pin-prick black pupils bore deep into his own. Its nose almost rubbed Marigold's and flecks of stringy, animal mucus coated his thinned beard as it snorted. There was rage in those eyes.

"Four of the cunts?" Marigold panted.

No. Neck was pulling his dagger from his throat, and Three was stomping along behind him.

This was Eyes, back already. Hag-faced shithead had healed himself in a matter of damn seconds.

"Of course you are! Of course you're magical, pissing skags!"

Eyes' mouth opened and lunged. Huge, broken fangs dripped with stinking strings of spit. Marigold faced momentary bewilderment as he found his face intact after the snap. His calves felt tight, his knees crashed into the floor. Three had pulled Marigold's legs out from beneath him. A fine stroke of luck for him that these cretins didn't have the mental faculties to fight together.

Marigold struggled to push himself to all fours as meaty fists and forearms from Eyes and Three rained down onto his back. Neck returned. Marigold saw his dagger fall to the ground between the stars in his vision. Two more fists joined in with the drumming up above. They could fucking carry on with it; if nothing else, Marigold had a strong back. He weathered the beatings whilst the skags seemed occupied with it, giving him time to send an exploratory hand out between the tangle of lumpy legs to retrieve his dagger. The bloodied weapon slipped in his hands as he angled the pointy end towards the skags. Up it went, into the space of Three that would have been filled with the bollocks of a man. The lack of reproductive organs didn't dampen the effect of the attack, though. Three fell backwards with the second ragged bellow of the fight, hitting the floor with a thud and surprising Neck and Eyes long enough for Marigold to roll away from his beating and grab Sear.

Marigold leapt up from the ground, rolled his shoulders to work out the kinks, and fixed his arms so that Sear was pointed directly at the trio. It was his turn to charge.

Sear split Neck's belly with ease. Bellow three. Intestines slopped out from the gash as Marigold twisted the blade, crunching bone and tearing vitals. From behind, Three wrapped its claws around Marigold's throat. Again, with the strangling. Neck tottered away from Marigold, Sear still lodged inside its gut. Perhaps "Sheath" would have been a better name for it. Eyes assaulted from the front, crashing headfirst into Marigold's stomach with the force of a charging rukh. The two skags and the warrior tripped and stumbled across the room and slammed into the curved wall. Marigold's back was saved by Three's fleshy chest, but his front felt like it had been caved in by Eyes' head. Amidst spluttering and gasping, Marigold reached down into the hairy, fleshy mass behind him and managed to yank the dagger clean from Three's nether regions. Eyes gathered itself and stood before Marigold, grinning idiotically. Marigold forced the dagger so far back through Eyes left eye that it poked out of the other side. The fourth bellow, and the second from Eyes. Poor bastard.

"Gimme another minute, Eyes."

Marigold twisted within Three's grasp, careful not to snap his own neck, and smashed an elbow into its clammy chest. Three made a sound like a split walrus. Must have broken a rib with that. It was enough for the moment of respite he needed.

Marigold freed himself and ran towards Neck. He kicked into the ripped abdomen. Blood spurted from the healing – but still ragged – slice. Marigold claimed Sear once more. He pivoted on the spot and cut through the air. There was a brief gag from Three before its head rolled from its neck and bounced across the stone. Three's body fell to its knees, then flat on its chest. A pool of dark blood gushed out across the floor. Good.

A rough fist caught the side of Marigold's face.

In what felt like slow motion, Marigold watched as a tooth – his fucking tooth – flew through the air before him, followed by a cloud of blood forced out between his pursed lips.

Eyes was back. Again.

Neck was up as well. The wound across its belly was just an angry red line now. What the fuck had Cezare done to these pricks? Neck's jagged teeth sunk into Marigold's arm as Eyes' rough arms caught him reeling from the punch. More scars to add to the collection.

Marigold dumped Sear again. No room to swing the bitch now. With his free arm, he pulled the knife from Eyes' head and thrust quick stabs at its chest. Air wheezed out from holes in the punctured lungs beneath. He twisted and sunk the blade into the side of Neck's head and left it there. As he rolled back, he caught sight of a bulbous mass emerging from the neck of Three, and a smaller shape developing beneath the head that lay on one side.

"I took your fucking head!" he gasped as he scrambled, once again, towards Sear.

Well, it was time for Sear to live up to her name.

There she was, back in his hands again. Dropped for the last time. He needed to treat her with the respect a woman deserved. As the three – soon to be four – skags began to regroup, Marigold plucked a small, glass vial from his belt and slid it into the bottom of Sear's hilt. He snapped the pommel shut and pushed it in. A click and a faint shattering echoed from within, and Marigold let the tip rest on the stones. Clear, viscous liquid coursed out from the wide hilt, down along the grooves cut into the vast slab of metal that was Sear's edge.

"Can you regrow ash?" he asked his new friends.

Marigold dashed the blade on the flagstones. Sparks flew as the floor refused to yield to metal. With a roar, Sear burst into raging flame.

Eyes and Neck were visibly taken aback by the sight, while the decapitated body of Three was pushing itself back up onto its knees; the new head had a mouth and lower nose, but nothing above yet. This wasn't Three anymore, this was Four! Eyes was the first to snarl in outrage, granting Neck a little more confidence. They lumbered back towards the waiting warrior.

Marigold held Sear out and barked a rough laugh, beating his barrel-chest with his free hand. The air around him rippled and warped with the heat.

Sear slid into Eyes' neck like a hot knife through butter. The flesh around it began to crackle and bubble as Marigold tightened every muscle in his arms and dragged the blade downwards. The liquid on the blade shook off onto Eyes' skin, melting flesh where it landed. Turns out cooked skag smelt worse than raw skag. Sear cut downwards, to the bottom of the beast. She rang out against the stone below like a church bell. Blood and viscera hissed and spat on the scorching blade as the two halves of Eyes splayed and fell to the ground, still attached by the unsplit top of the head. Marigold pulled back and swung again. Another hit. Neck's head flew across the room, and before it could even land Marigold hacked the remaining body another four times. The second skag was ablaze.

Three's head had grown a remarkable amount of new body, but had nothing more than baby legs down below. His new pal, Four, was just about fighting fit on his brother's old body. Four, being a new head, obviously had no memories of what had gone down in the fight so far. Perhaps foolishly, it rushed towards its new foe with all the gusto of beginning a fresh battle. The moron happily tried to eat Sear. Through its teeth Sear smashed, and down its pink gullet she raced. The luckless twat fell forwards, admitting the rest of her with ease. Four's head began to cook from within. Marigold drew Sear from her skag scabbard and the new challenger slumped heavily to the ground, smoking from the mouth.

By this point, Three was dragging itself across the stones, away from Marigold and giving up on the pathetic legs it pulled behind it. Skags weren't particularly intelligent beasts, but it seemed that this one knew it had lost the fight. It *had* just watched its previous body go up in flame. That couldn't be pleasant for anybody to witness.

"Where do you think you're going to go?" Marigold taunted, walking alongside the terrified beast as it circled the room on its belly. The fuel in Sear's hilt was almost spent. As much fun as it was to draw the fight out now that he was on the winning side of it, fire was the only thing that was going to end it. Marigold had three more vials on his belt, but this tower was a veritable cloud-scraper, and he didn't want his deck to run out of aces just yet. "Hope you got everything you wanted out of life, my friend."

Marigold dropped the white-hot blade through the top of Three's skull. It's arms and malformed legs shook in random directions for a few moments before the creature fell silent. Marigold left Sear swaying gently within the skag so that the last of her flames could find a new home on the grey flesh.

"Now that was a fight," he grinned. He looked around the room as he stood with his hands on his knees. "Door's still fucking locked though." He tongued the new gap in his teeth, thoughtfully.

As if in answer, a small, metal object clattered to the ground beneath the burnt husk of Eyes.

Marigold bent down to investigate. He found a black piece of metal, still hot to the touch. It quite obviously had the cut of a key, but was nowhere near big enough to fit the lock of the gate. He sat cross-legged and studied the object. As he scraped away the blackened blood and flesh, he found grooves and pegs along the piece.

"Three domes, three skags... By Greldin, what a fucking puzzle."

Ruefully, he glanced over at the smouldering shapes of Neck and Four. It was grim work, but it needed to be done.

Marigold was up to his elbows in cooked skag by the time he retrieved the second and third pieces. He smeared the mess on his jerkin and began to fit the parts together. Sure enough, it was a key. What a fucking runabout. Did Cezare want him up there or not? Let him go on floor two, chucked him a puzzle that could easily have gone unsolved on floor three. Three-and-a-half shitting skags, but he couldn't say that he hadn't enjoyed it. It had almost been enough for him to forget why he had come here in the first place. Almost.

The three-part key slid easily into its hole in the lock, despite the chunks of skag flesh that were baked onto it. The hefty clasp snapped open and the door swung outwards. Marigold collected Sear — now sufficiently cooled — and slid her into the scabbard on his back. He took his dagger from the cauterised head of Neck and kicked its charred skull around the room on his way back to the newly unlocked staircase. He crushed it underfoot before heading up.

Chapter Four

FLIGHT OF FANCY

Another floor above, another twisting spiral of ill-cut steps to stumble up. Marigold took three-a-stride, racing up to the next trial that Cezare had so lovingly planned out for him. If he was honest with himself, he was actually looking forward to it. The euphoria of the previous fight was yet to fade, and the blood was yet to dry.

Light bloomed ahead.

Marigold felt a wet slap on the back of his neck as he leapt out of the shaft. He would have been more concerned with what that might have been were he not instead taken aback by the clear blue skies and far-reaching plains of wild grass that met him. He furrowed his brow as he spun around to look back at the way he had come. Where was the stone? Where was the...

Where was what? What was he looking for again?

"Chief, just look at it! It's incredible!"

Vik sidled up alongside Marigold, bobbing slightly on his rukh, Hilda. Marigold stared at Vik, then at the feathered rump of Gretel beneath his own legs. Confusion began to fade as he realised that Sieg and silent Haggar were also trotting nearby on their own birds.

They had travelled so far to kill it, and there it finally was.

Far ahead, tearing through the trees on the distant edge of the plain was the magnificent dragon, Nidhogg, the greatest of all beasts in Rosaria. Resplendent in bright red scales that caught the sun, snaking through the forest on its gleaming, yellow underbelly, casting immense shadows over the plains with its outstretched wings as big as a village. The snow-capped mountains beyond only served to make it stand out even more.

"It's the biggest I've ever fucking seen," laughed Sieg. "And you really think we can take it?"

"Of course we can, lads," roared Marigold. "But let's make sure we don't scare the fucker away before we reach it!" It wasn't the first time he had taken on something that was ridiculously bigger than he, and if he had his way it most certainly wouldn't be the last. He kicked at Gretel's rump and the bird burst into action, hammering the ground as she took the lead, rushing towards the monstrous wyrm.

Haggar flashed his teeth and nodded at Marigold as he caught up. Haggar didn't speak much. Haggar didn't have a tongue. Most of Marigold's clan had heroic tales to tell about their wounds and scars. Haggar had lost his tongue in an altercation between some booze and a flaming torch. It turned out that he hadn't been able to breathe fire, and now he couldn't tell the tale, either.

"Oh no you bloody don't, that beast is mine!" Marigold laughed at his mute friend.

"Fuck me, lads, wait! Just wait, you bastards!" Vik cried faintly from behind. "Hilda's not as young as your birds!"

"You didn't have to bring her out here," cried Sieg, gripping tightly around the base of his own rukh's neck. He had almost caught up to Marigold. "Fucking perfect weather for it," he hollered, standing in his saddle, madly waving his axe in the air.

The plains were vast, but the Rukhs killed the distance between them and the dragon quickly. This was their turf. Open grassland was what rukhs were born to run on. They hurtled towards Marigold's mark. In response, it threw its boxy head up into the air, spouting flames from cave-like nostrils. Its ear-rending screech threatened to knock the men clear from their mounts.

Marigold screamed instructions at the top of his lungs to the men, but he couldn't even hear his own voice inside his head beneath the din. The enormous wings of the monster began to beat, their size so great that it appeared that the dragon was moving in slow motion while the world around it carried on at a normal pace. The oversized lizard was trying to escape without a fight. The biggest Marigold had seen, and yet still there was a hint of the coward about it.

Nidhogg was above them now, talons the size of tower spires hanging overhead as the claws that flexed them lifted from the ground. Unfortunately for the dragon, it owned a tail longer than some men managed to travel in their lives. It snaked along the ground behind the lumbering beast, struggling to join the rest of the body in the air as it caught on trees and rocks. Marigold stood atop Gretel, balancing with his arms held aloft. As the end of the bright yellow tail whipped past him, Marigold leapt from his rukh and wrapped his tree-trunk arms around the scaly appendage. Sieg and Haggar followed suit, Sieg using his knives to hook a hold into a thicker chunk of the dragon.

Marigold, Sieg, and Haggar were lifted high up into the air. Vik flailed his arms wildly below, no doubt cursing and screaming at missing out on the action after coming all this way. Marigold chuckled as he swung himself up onto the top of the tail. They were actually on the monstrosity, on the King of the Beasts. But, they were far from done with their hunt. Nidhogg's tail whipped the air frantically. The dragon knew the men were on it. The grass below was torn away as the dragon fled up into the skies. The trees, the plains, the mountains... Everything shrunk in size. In its rage, the dragon belched forth a spray of flame down upon the land below. Marigold and his remaining men looked down in dismay as he saw the fires engulf Vik and all of their rukhs. They both turned to Marigold, staring in wide-eyed silence.

"Shit. Vik wasn't pretty before, and he certainly won't be pretty now. We'll tell the clan that he died with us, on the beast," he cried back above the din of rushing wind. "We might have a meal of roast rukh when we're done, though."

Sieg and Haggar nodded at their chief. The trio continued their deadly ascent along the scales of Nidhogg.

They were up within the clouds by the time they reached the heaving muscles that flapped and controlled Nidhogg's titanic wings. All three of them had unravelled lengths of rope and climbing spikes from their waists. They stabbed metal in and heaved it out as they slowly picked their way up. The dragon seemed utterly unconcerned with the minor wounds the group made on their ascent. Perhaps it believed it had shaken them off?

The skies were ice up at this height. Marigold, feverish at the prospect of bringing down the grandest beast of them all, was nonetheless pleased that the clouds beneath them hid the details of the drop to the ground, far below; they were going to bring the dragon down, which meant they were coming down with it. The wings slowed their beating, Nidhogg held them out and began to glide calmly through the skies. Where in Rosaria were they by now?

What did it matter?

They were on the neck now. The squarish head was just ahead, bobbing up and down with the effort of controlling those colossal wings. Ivory horns protruded from countless locations between the scales, some as thick as a tower, others creating an excellent path for Marigold and his lads to clamber through. It was like a forest of spines up here. How in the fucking Pits were they going to bring this arsehole down? Bastard didn't seem like it was thinking about landing any time soon, either, and Marigold rather fancied the prospect of food and drink and tales this night. Preferably in lands he knew his way around.

They reached the head, struggling to stand straight amidst the force of the rushing wind. Nevertheless, they were still unnoticed by the dragon. They each looked between one another, hoping that one of them had something resembling a plan.

Haggar was the first to pipe up, though with hands rather than voice. He tore his spike from the flesh of the monster and staggered through the horns and wind to the edge of the head. He gestured down with the hand that was clutching the spike. He held an arm above and below his head and looked left and right.

"An eye?" Sieg asked at the top of his lungs. His voice was tiny.

Haggar nodded.

"Could've just pointed at your fucking eye!" Marigold yelled back.

Haggar shrugged his shoulders, then buried the metal point of his climbing spike deep into side of the dragon's head.

At that moment, the clouds broke.

Haggar, thrown by the sight of such an immense drop, teetered perilously over the edge. Nidhogg banked left, tipping the mute barbarian off. Marigold and Sieg clung desperately to their own embedded lifelines. From between the gnarled horns Marigold saw Haggar's spike jerk downwards. He hadn't let go. Good man.

The dragon levelled out. Marigold crawled over the enormous head and peered over the side. There was Haggar, clinging on for dear life, bouncing back and forth against the black eye of the beast. He kicked off the boulder-sized sphere in an attempt to climb up. The dragon bellowed, louder than the wind itself. Flames spewed ahead. It twisted in the air, banking right. Marigold was thrown away. Sieg's strong hand gripped his arm and pulled him back onto the head before he was forced to try flying all by himself. Nidhogg's raging seemed to subside. Marigold and Sieg scrambled back to locate Haggar.

An empty rope whipped the skies.

"Fuck!" Sieg cried.

"Fuck this fucking worm," yelled Marigold.

Without another word, Sieg began hauling the rope up. He wrapped it around his shoulders and waist and, with a glare of determination and a nod at Marigold, leapt over the edge with his own spike firmly in hand. Marigold almost cast himself over as he rushed to watch his friend fall. Sieg landed directly on the middle of the eye, spike-point first.

The dragon roared again, its agony clearly announced to the world.

A cascade of clear fluid showered forth. Sieg disappeared between the torn membrane that flapped against the skies. The end of the rope slithered out from the eye. Empty again. The dragon plunged into a spiral.

Marigold thrust his spike back into the red head, wrapping his legs around Haggar's spike, gripping both for dear life. Tears streamed from his windswept eyes. Sieg had done a grand fucking number on the Nidhogg from within. Good lad. Shame he hadn't been the one to make the killing blow though, and that this was likely to be the end of them both.

The distant earth hurtled closer. Clouds faded around man and beast. Green masses became individual trees. Paths developed within the land.

It was a good way to die.

Nidhogg shattered its head on the earth, teeth first. Marigold felt a majestic snap from within the dragon's neck as vertebrae crumbled. The shockwave from the monster was almost enough to throw him from his spike. Earth and trees and dust were flung up into the air as Nidhogg carved a ravine through the land. Its great wings were shredded as they scraped along behind it. The right one tore off completely, causing Nidhogg to begin a slow turn as the momentum it had picked up began to die along with the creature itself.

Nidhogg and Marigold stopped moving.

Marigold looked at his hands. The first thing to note was that they were still attached to his arms, and the small matter of him being able to see suggested that his head still remained attached to his shoulders.

He was alive.

The dirt settled. The land settled. A silence seemed to descend over Marigold and the slain dragon. Marigold let go of the spike. His fingers were white. He was fucking alive!

"Sieg!" he shouted. "Sieg? Where are you, you beautiful cocksucker?"

There was no answer.

Slowly but surely, Marigold picked his way to the wide snout of Nidhogg, lowering himself to the ground with his rope. He ran out of rope and had to drop the last distance. He cried out for his friend once more.

The biggest dragon there ever was lay dead, sprawled out over who knew how far. A huge portion of tongue twitched on the dirt below the mouth, bitten off in the moment the jaw had slammed into the teeth above. Might make a decent trophy, if he still had someone to help him carry it.

There was another movement. A struggling within the flaccid remains of Nidhogg's burst eye. An arm! A head! Sieg slid out on a flow of juice, crumpling to the floor below, drenched in viscera. Marigold ran over to his man. Shit, he was in a bad state. Bones ripped through both legs. He was missing a hand that ended in a charred stump, and the other arm was obviously broken. Marigold wiped the gore from Sieg's face. Eyes blinked beneath it. Sieg didn't move his head, but he looked towards his chief.

"Fucking did it, though, didn't we?" Sieg gasped, and closed his eyes.

"You did it," Marigold soothed. "You killed the cunt, you fucking madman."

Sieg said no more.

But this was strange. Unreal. As Marigold held Sieg's broken body in his arms, he couldn't help but feel like he had been through this death before. And it wasn't a death brought about at the talons of a damned dragon.

Sieg was already dead. In fact, so was Haggar. And Vik. They'd all died with knives in their throats. But where? Why?

Think.

The tower! Tower? The mage! Cezare! Cezare was behind it all. And he was on his way to settling the score. He'd been in the tower. His head pounded something rotten as he forced dreams and reality apart, struggling to decide which was real.

Abruptly, Marigold realised that he was finding it difficult to move his arms. He watched in astonishment as the massive carcass of Nidhogg began to fade away, as the dirt and the skies and the grasses were replaced with darkness and stone. He stared at his wrists as metal cuffs materialised around them. He studied them for a moment.

He was sat. And he was strapped to a fucking chair.

"Ah no, this is no good. No good at all." An unknown and high-pitched voice trembled from somewhere in the dank surroundings.

Marigold's head spontaneously directed itself at the source to see a white-haired and white-cloaked man with an arched back pottering around the side of him. He held a writhing black mass in his gloved hands. "And just who in the damned Pits are you?" he asked.

"Why, I'm Cezare's Bloodmaster. Don't worry yourself, Marigold." He nudged thin, circular glasses further up his nose. "I've been instructed to make sure your death is peaceful. Now, I'll just replace your leech with this one." He held the squirming black blob closer to Marigold's face. "Your other one filled up rather quickly. Lots of blood for it to feast on, just what we like to see."

"What pissing leech are on you about?"

"Cezare requires your blood, my good man, and you are far too formidable one-on-one, so we decided that it was would be best for all involved if we took the necessary precautions."

Marigold felt a sharp tug at the back of his head as the Bloodmaster pulled what was evidently a full leech from him.

"Did you have a good dream? I've used smaller leeches for my own purposes. Recreational, you understand! Such grand dreams. Feel almost real, don't they?"

"I had a fucking fantastic dream," Marigold answered honestly. He looked at the metal cuffs around both of his wrists. They were metal, but they were attached to an old, wooden chair. A barbarian, strapped to a wooden chair. He shook his head derisively. "Amateurs."

"Beg your pardon?"

Marigold's chair did the answering. Splintering wood flew as the occupant wrenched his arms free of their pathetic bonds. The semi-circle straps of metal over his wrists bounced on the stones as the Bloodmaster dropped his leeches in horror. Marigold gripped the sides of the wiry man's head. The wriggling blood-suckers hit the floor with a wet splat at roughly the same moment the Bloodmaster's skull popped.

Marigold launched himself up from his unwanted seat, tearing the rest of it to smithereens in the process. He shook the blood and pink brain matter from his hands, and stomped upon the fattest of the two leeches. He watched with satisfaction as a spray of blood spurted out from beneath his boot. Well, that was actually his blood. He grimaced. Marigold took a moment to take in his surroundings. It certainly seemed that he was back in the tower. Circular room, a little narrower than the previous three. Two slit windows on either side left the space dark and dingy, the only decent light coming from an array of candles that stood dripping over tables strewn with blood-filled vials and jars that churned with more of those bloody leeches. The musty smell was so thick it almost served as a meal. Marigold picked up one of the jars and held it up to his face. Four or five of the wriggling bastards swam within a hazy, yellow liquid. He tipped the thing over the Bloodmaster's corpse. They could damn well suck on that.

"Cezare!" he hollered into the room. "Your 'Bloodmaster's' going to need replacing. Things kind of came to a head." He was pleased with that one.

There was no response from the proprietor of the tower, but Marigold didn't doubt that he was listening. Was this also part of the plan? Was he meant to escape this floor, or was four intended to be his end? Fucking leeches, though. Another new one. This Cezare was full of tricks, and the confirmation of a blood requirement almost certainly meant that he was dealing with a Summoner. Summoners meant demons, and that was no good for anybody. He had to thank the cunt though; the fabricated memories of Nidhogg were going to stick with him for a long time, and they were a far better way to remember the deaths of his closest friends than the only ones he had previously owned.

What the fuck even was a dragon?

Chapter Five

IT'S WHAT'S INSIDE THAT COUNTS

Marigold could hear chains clinking together above, dangling free or holding something that swung. It didn't sound good. More skags? The last steps of the spiral glistened with the small amount of light that seeped inside the passage. Wet. Marigold's boots slipped into the corner of the shiny steps.

Blood.

He pushed his thick arms against the walls of the chamber, steadying himself, and carefully clambered each of the last few steps one at a time. What a sight that must be; a huge man tiptoeing upstairs. Still, it gave him plenty of time to examine what was awaiting him on the next floor.

Bodies.

Bodies chained by their feet to the ceiling. Dangling arms reached for the slick stones beneath them. Circular glyphs were cut deep into their chests. Naked and bloodied, and all of them dead. And they weren't just any bodies, either. Already, from the first chain that swayed gently before him, he recognised the battered and upturned face as one of the farmers that had been complaining about his missing goats. Old Ivar. Just behind him swung his wife, Helene. Here were the missing clansmen. Those he hoped had escaped the camp. Were all of these bodies his people? What in the Pits did Cezare have against them all to have done this?

As Marigold stepped up out of the twisting stairs, the stench hit him. Vicious and overpowering. The metallic smell dug deep into his nostrils. Marigold hacked and coughed to clear his lungs, disturbing a heaving mass of flies as he staggered into the room. His eyes were filled with the black swarm, his ears assaulted by their buzzing cacophony. He wafted his arms about to clear the air. The horde billowed this way and that, some becoming stuck on the tacky floor, others returning to the bodies, and – thank the Pits – a great deal of them fled out through the numerous slit windows, into the early afternoon sky. This was too much like his ruined camp for comfort.

Marigold remained still, forcing himself to get used to the smell. He had to press on. It wasn't the first time he had found himself in a space filled with blood by any means and, if he had his way, the next time after this would be coming very fucking soon. But no matter how strong his stomach was in situations like this, knowing that it was his own clan members creating the smell was not something that was easy to deal with. Especially not as it was the second time today. The lust for Cezare's life grew stronger. His blood would smell sweet, it would gush like a river in a storm.

Ivar and Helene weren't the only ones he knew here. Gunnar, Rolf, Sigurd; all fine warriors. Lisbeth, Marie, Bjørg; all fine wives. He pushed through into the middle of the room. Sear's hilt caught in the crotch of Margit. The chains above groaned as Marigold freed himself. Three Eriks. Nils, Olaf and Tor; fuck, they were barely adults. Vidar and Kjell; he'd taught them to hunt. Karin; he'd taught her to ride a rukh. There were so many of them hanging that Marigold found himself unable to see the other side of the room. Thank Greldin that his wife was safely buried and not chained among them. The flies continued their graceless flights, bumbling into bodies, landing on the remnants of Marigold's beard, crunching underfoot.

"How the shit did those maggots take you down?" he asked the enormous body of Magnus, at what he believed to be the middle of the room.

Marigold was surrounded. He wasn't scared, but this was far from pleasant. He was going to have to bury all of them. Hard work. Work that would have to come later. He silently apologised to his friends and began to push through in the direction that he assumed the next set of stairs to be in.

A tearing sound came from behind.

Marigold spun, bodies swung heavily around him as Sear pushed them aside. Dead weights knocked him off-balance as he stumbled back through the room to investigate. Skin began to rip, sinews snapped, bones cracked. The sounds of a fight that Marigold wasn't yet involved in.

"The fuck have you dumped in here with me, Cezare?" he growled.

Only the ear-rending sounds of violence continued.

"Answer me, you fucking cock boil, or are you all out of spells?"

A fine mist of blood hissed from the torso of the body of Frode as it writhed ahead of Marigold. The spray covered the barbarian's face. Another layer of grime. Marigold held the body still within his huge hands, and twisted it savagely to catch out whatever was on the other side.

The back was clear. Cut up and bleeding, but clear.

Hastily, Marigold searched the sticky floor beneath the bodies. He lowered his head below the dangling arms and scanned the small, clear space below the hanging massacre. Nothing but flies and gore. He straightened back up, kneeling in the blood, and a tiny, sharp-nailed hand burst out from between the ribs of Frode. Marigold jerked back as the red-skinned, three-fingered hand clutched at the air, narrowly missing his closest eye.

"What in the pissing Pits have we got here?" he asked the creature that struggled beneath Frode's ruined chest. An angry red stripe appeared at the bottom of Frode's ribs and tore upwards. The frantic hand was joined by a second, then the shiny sphere of a bald head pushed through. Marigold waited patiently for the creature to sort itself out. The head emerged in full. It snapped back, upside down, and glared at Marigold with pure black eyes. Countless jagged teeth filled the tiny mouth as it stretched wide and screeched at Marigold. It was remarkably fucking similar to the little shits that he had found in pieces around his wrecked camp. Marigold snaked his thick fingers around the neck of the demonic bastard and wrenched it clear from Frode's ragged chest. Shredded lungs and fountains of blood gushed over Marigold's feet, but as he casually twisted the head from the puny neck of the creature – no bigger than a baby – he saw something else inside Frode's chest cavity. An oval. Swirling at the edges but otherwise a clear window to a hell-scape of red sand, jagged rocks, and dark, bubbling skies.

"Ah, so it *is* the Pits," he concluded, throwing down the two separate pieces of the demon.

The fucking Pits.

Marigold had no idea where the Pits were, or which one in particular this was. The Pits were the planes that demons and other assorted gribblies walked. Violent lands of fighting and blood and evil. The Pits were the realms that kept children awake long into the night after they demanded the most gruesome of stories from their parents. Marigold thought that he would probably enjoy a brief trip there sometime, but perhaps not right now while he still had work to do in his own plane. What rancid plan had Cezare dreamed up? Summoning an army of fragile fucking demons to do his bidding? Had that pus-filled, hex-casting, cock-sucking son of a hag bitch butchered his family, ended his closest friends, and ravaged his clan for this? He concentrated on the pathetic remains of the imp at his feet.

He felt rage boiling within.

The tell-tale tearing sounds that had begun this investigation sprung up from several places around the room.

The portal inside Frode still churned.

"I'm sorry, friend." Marigold wrapped his arms around the ribs and crushed. Warmth ran down his front as ribs and vertebrae cracked and snapped. Frode's mangled corpse hung at an awkward angle, but the portal was gone.

Pattering tapped the wet floor at several points around the warrior. The rending sounds began from within other bodies.

Marigold unsheathed Sear once more. "Come on then, you stack of cunts."

The impish onslaught began.

Two leapt from chained body to chained body, like red, hairless monkeys. They sailed through the air, screeching as they latched onto Marigold's shoulders with their tiny teeth and claws. Before he could even see to those, three more of the scabby shits were gnawing at his shins, groping up towards his stones.

"Oh no you fucking don't!" Marigold booted the one standing on his shoe away. It sailed through the space between swinging bodies, crashing spine-first into the back of a swinging head. The two on his shoulders sunk their teeth into his neck. Marigold bellowed, and grabbed one of them. He dragged it off, its nails scraping three gouges across the back of his head as it scrabbled for purchase. Marigold ripped the little horror in half.

More tearing. More dropping. More pattering. Squeals of ear-piercing delight began to burst out from within the tears in the hanging bodies.

"How bloody many of you are there?"

It was time to put an end to these swirls from another realm; he was going to have to tear these bodies up, for there was no space to swing a sword. Yet. He dropped Sear back into her sheath. His fingernails dug deep into swinging flesh. Thick blood leaked over them as his knuckles sunk inside. Marigold found purchase deep within and pulled. Wet slopping accompanied his actions as he pulled his arms clean from the body, fingers wrapped tightly around broken shards of rib. The skeleton within collapsed under the assault, while chest, shoulders, and head slumped to the floor. Best not to look at the face.

The bottom of the twirling and red mass buried deep inside vanished as soon as it was revealed. Entrails and gore slopped about Marigold's feet. He shook his hands to shake them clean of the excess. Chunks of flesh remained stuck beneath his nails. Foul work, but it needed to be done.

He grabbed the next body and did the same.

And the next.

And the next.

Marigold was held fast in a blood-induced frenzy. A space was beginning to clear. Enough to invite Sear out into. As Marigold's hands went to the hilt reaching up from his back, a thick and slimy pressure wrapped itself about Marigold's belly.

"Snakes?" he panicked. Marigold hated snakes. Hissing, dead-eyed fucks wouldn't think twice about sinking their fangs into you whether you wanted to attack them or not.

The grip tightened. Marigold let go of Sear's hilt for what felt like the hundredth fucking time and looked down. He had just a moment to see that it wasn't in fact a snake but some kind of suckered tentacle before he was yanked off his feet and dragged backwards.

Marigold's head cracked against the floor.

Immediately his fingers grappled around for a gap in the stones, but the blood and gore coating those and his fingers left nothing but a slippery mess with nothing to hold. He seized one of the bodies above, holding on with everything he had, the head of the unfortunate fellow pressed into his. The pressure around his waist tightened. Suckers dug in and pulled. The body he clung to tore from its chains and Marigold dropped heavily to the ground. Only the feet of his erstwhile friend remained swinging gently above.

The slick floor transported Marigold quickly. The tentacle, thick as his thigh, was retreating into a gaping wound in one of the bodies. "You'll have a fucking job pulling me through that, you fat, suckered cock," he yelled, nevertheless trying to wrap his fingers around the tentacle, eager to prise the damn thing off. The shitting thing was just too slippery. Two of the impish folk that had been materialising from the other bodies leapt onto his chest. "And it gets pissing worse," he snarled, grasping each of them by their necks and slamming them into one another as the group was dragged along. A grey paste fell from the meeting point, and he hurled the carcasses at the torso that contained the blubbery tentacle. The creature on the other side – whatever it was – yanked hard. Marigold's skull lurched, once again beating against the floor beneath it. His hands trailed behind him. Between the stars in his eyes, he looked back to see several pairs of feet touch down on the ground that now appeared to be the ceiling. "Fuck, fuck, fuck!"

Then, he stopped moving with a harsh jerk.

His body became rigid as he realised he was now being pulled in two directions at once. He found his hands entangled with two smaller tentacles, stretching out from somewhere, from corpses out of sight. One of the imps fell from above onto Marigold's chest, digging down and scrambling into the torn arm of his jerkin. Out of fucking sight, but the nips and scratches told him just where the bastard was. Marigold strained. A lesser man would have been ripped asunder by now, but Marigold at least had muscle and brawn on his side. If these Pit-spawned tentacles were going to tear him limb from limb, they were going to have to put all they had into it. With everything he could muster, Marigold tried to tighten himself into a ball, or at least the closest shape that would resemble it. Sharp bites came from beneath his clothes. Great, bass groans rippled from the ruined body ahead, the source of the tentacle around his waist. The bastards were both right there with him and a whole dimension away at once. Best not to dwell on how that worked. Chains clunked and groaned as all three of the slimy worms pulled for all their worth.

Deadlock, but Marigold wasn't planning on giving up.

The thick tentacle slid further through into the realm of men, splaying the ribs around it further outwards.

"Come on, cunt, do my fucking work for me." The imp within his clothing bit hard on something sensitive. "Do it now," he howled.

Further out it came. Cracks and pops and slops filled the air as viscera squirted this way and that. The tentacles around Marigold's wrists began sliding up his arms, flicking his ears and short, rough-cut hair. He knew it had been a good idea to cut the bloody stuff off. Marigold heaved one more time, dragging the fat fucker out as far as the body could withstand. The head and shoulders below the length of the unknown beast tore away and dropped and, with the body destroyed, the portal within winked out of existence. The tentacle was sliced off at the source. Body and beast crashed to the deck. A ruined lung spilled out of the mess as the tentacle writhed around for a few moments before releasing its grip around Marigold's stomach. A roar of definite agony cried out from the remaining portals in the body. Either the fucker was one massive creature, or the other tentacles belonged to something else that was very close by. Marigold raised his back up with scrabbling legs and threw himself back down onto the wriggling arsehole within his clothes. A spread of warmth on his back signalled a victory there. Slowly but surely, the tide was turning in Marigold's favour.

With only his hands bound, Marigold spun around, twisting the tentacles together into some unholy braid of oily flesh. He yanked towards himself, got a better idea of where the bodies holding these pricks were. One each side of the circular room. Typical. It wasn't the first time he'd had his hands bound, and it was unlikely to be the last, but it was usually on his own terms. Or his wife's. There was nothing else for it. He bit into the writhing mass.

Marigold gagged.

The flesh, not of this world, tasted like nothing else Marigold had ever had the displeasure of shifting between teeth and tongue. Hot, thick liquid filled his mouth, scalding the insides of his cheek, burning his taste buds. He spat the chunk out and bit again. And again. The twisted creature tried to unravel itself, but instead just stretched further. One more chomp and Marigold was held by only one fleshy string. The wounded member slithered back across the room, back to its host. Marigold, his arms held together by the tangled mess he had made himself, spun his arms in a wide circle, wrapping the last tentacle about them. If he couldn't use his hands, he'd use his whole fucking body. He heard the familiar tearing of flesh and bone, then felt the pressure around his wrist disappear as another thud hit the ground.

The room cleared of demonic chatterings. Clinking chains, dripping blood, and hunks of soft, dead flesh bumping into one another caressed Marigold's ears.

"Finally, some bloody peace."

If the room had been a state before he had arrived in it, it was a vision of the End Times now. Body parts strewn everywhere, pieces of imp garnishing the gore, not a brick unspattered with dark blood. Two tentacles from a plane of existence Marigold thought he would rather forget glistened in the low light, one of them still twitched a little. The flies, scattered by the furore, descended once more, feasting on man and creature alike. Surely it really was no worse than the Pits in here now. Marigold puffed his lips out at the sight, the air whistling through the recent gap left in his gums.

He began to check himself over. He'd had to accept a fair few cuts and bruises in this altercation. Beneath his jerkin were welts, angry and red. Reminders of where the tentacles had gripped the hardest. All over his arms and legs were the minute engravings gifted to him by the narrow nails of the imps that had dropped from the bodies. His back hurt like a bastard, and the sweat dripping down it wasn't helping matters one bit. It was probably for the best that he couldn't see exactly what had gone on back there. As he shrugged around inside his clothes, the final piece of the little shit that had been in there fell out, sticking to the blood pool on the stone below. A finger. Fantastic.

Marigold drew Sear from his back. Finally, he had some space to work with. He strode around the room, thrusting the blade through each body that didn't have an open chest or back wound. A simple task, and one that would hopefully mark the end of any more surprises from within. There wasn't much left to clean his weapon on, so he had to content himself with the least bloodied rag that hung from the arse of one of the dead village women. He apologised to the corpse, for the intrusion and the gaping gash in her torso, just in case there was a grudge blossoming on the other side at this moment.

Wearily, Marigold sheathed Sear and pushed through the swinging forest of bodies. He arrived at the next set of steps, sliding a touch on the slick blood that covered the flags before them. He looked back over the room once more before he left.

"Fuck me," he sighed.

THE REWARD

"Oh, it's big. It's very white. And it is certainly a beast," Marigold growled, listing the chief characteristics of their quarry. "But this is not a fucking gargunnoch."

The sun beat down from the clear blue skies. Marigold and his three accomplices stood around their slain quarry. Sear burned violently in Marigold's hand. The sea of grass surrounding them lapped gently against their shins in the light breeze, while the rukhs pecked nonchalantly at the dirt. Sieg and Haggar leaned on the side of the colossal creature as its final breaths wheezed out from the tens of puncture wounds decorating its side.

Vik's axe rang out as he yanked it from the flesh. A spurt of blood wet the side of his face with it. "Maybe they just got confused, Chief? You said it yerself, city folk wouldn't know a fucking gargunnoch if it sucked them off." He licked the blood from his mouth, then spat it out with a grimace.

"Vik." Marigold let his head drop to one side. He thrust Sear at the bloodied, warty head that was almost as big as Marigold himself. "The cunt's got, what…" He tapped the point of his sword at the monster, "…one, two, three, four… five, six… seven, eight! Eight fucking eyes! Two of them are in the back of its shitting, fucking head!" He could feel his blood boiling. "Tell me, Vik, tell me of all the predators you know that have eyes in the back of their head. What bloody gargunnoch needs to see what's going on behind it? Who gets that wrong?"

"Chief, c'mon," Vik sighed. "We've brought it down, whatever it is. Does it really matter?"

Sieg muttered in agreement behind him.

Marigold wasn't finished yet. "Flat-fucking-teeth? Flat!" He lifted the lips below man-length grey tusks to reveal a line of yellow, brick-sized molars. Thick strings of saliva stretched from top to bottom, leaking out over gums and onto the undergrowth. "The only thing this has been terrorising is the fucking grass. Face it, boys, we've been bloody had, and I've wasted a perfectly good vial in Sear." He thrust his blade between the beast's ribs, dousing the flames.

"But Chief," Vik and Sieg offered in unison, while Haggar gestured in silent agreement.

"It's like Vik says, Chief," continued Sieg, "fucking thing's dead, who cares what it is? They won't know what it is now. If they thought this thing was a gargunnoch in the first place, they still will. Let's get the head to the city and claim our reward. Claim it before they really do work out what it is. And to be honest, Boss, you lit your sword up far too fucking early."

"Cut its cunt head off then." Marigold stormed away from the maw and paced around the remainder of the beast. It was at least as long as a gargunnoch was supposed to be. "You can carry it to the fucking city, though," he called back.

The lads got to work hacking and pulling. One of the rukhs reached over in curiosity, snapping at errant shreds of meat as they fell away from the carcass. Marigold occupied himself with examination of the beast. What in the Pits was it? He passed three legs on one side before he found himself inspecting the backside of the titan. A stumpy tail barely the length of Sear itself hung listlessly in the breeze. A real bloody gargunnoch had a tail longer than its body; it was one of their defining features. Marigold found his eyes drawn to a circular mark on the rump, small and red and just below its stinking arsehole. An irregular, scabby ring. A new scabby ring by the looks of it. That was not something he wanted to find at all.

"Vik, Sieg, Haggar!" he yelled.

The three of them ran to him, axes and knives gripped in each hand.

"Fucking thing's been summoned here." He pointed to the symbol. "Prick's not even likely from this plane, some veggie bastard dragged here from its own world against its will."

"Whatever, Boss, it's still dead," said Sieg simply. "It don't change a thing."

"And who do you suppose fucking summoned it?" Why couldn't they see? He sighed. The boys just had the reward in their sights. "Fine. Just don't be expecting that reward to come so easily, lads. We'll take the bloody head and we'll throw it over the fucking walls if we have to. Keep your weapons ready. This isn't right. None of it fucking is."

"Mari," Sieg said frankly, "I think we can deal with one little prick with a wand. Summoners summon because they can't fight."

Marigold couldn't deny that it was always good to maintain an air of confidence and a can-do attitude. In truth, it was commendable that his men took everything in their stride. Good that they saw no obstacle as insurmountable. But, it didn't make Marigold feel any easier about the situation.

Haggar wordlessly hoisted the hulking head onto the back of his rukh. The bird swayed beneath the burden, pecking violently at the air around it, as if that was somehow to blame for the indignation it was suffering. Marigold thought the creature would collapse altogether when Haggar swung himself on top with it. The man wasn't small, by any stretch of the imagination; had he a tongue in that mouth of his, he might have broken the bird's back.

The City of Hvitstein was not exactly the kind of place that Marigold was expecting.

White walls were punctuated by square towers. Trim grass grew neatly around the outside. A well-maintained moat had a wide, wooden drawbridge for a crossing. Two red flags rippled wildly, positively glowing against the pale background of snow-capped mountains beyond. It was almost exactly as Dahl had described it; a white city. Marigold had been sure it would be wooden-stake walls, bowmen, ropes, and a pot for boiling.

"Shall we go in then?" Sieg asked.

Vik just trotted along anyway. Haggar was lagging behind, his bird at the point of exhaustion beneath the obscene weight it was being forced to lug about.

A group of men, women, and children dressed in bright colours and puffy clothes were milling beneath the entrance arch. Marigold wasn't sure whether it was worth noting that none crossed the threshold. It was, after all, entirely possible that they still feared something lurking beyond their strong walls.

"I suppose that's the next step," he sighed, peering around warily. "Fine, come on, let's get this over and done with."

The city folk surrounded the four men and their rukhs as they trotted inside. Hands reached out, stroking feathers, grasping at thighs.

"They've done it."
"It's dead."
"They really did it."

"Heroes."

"We can play outside again."

Marigold looked at Vik. Vik looked at Sieg. Sieg looked at Haggar. Haggar drew the reins of his bird and halted. The crowd moved back a little as the huge mute slid out from his saddle and onto the dusty city street. He dragged the decapitated head from the back of his squawking rukh. It slopped to the ground and a spurt of blood formed an irregular ball in the grit.

"Listen, Hvitstein. Your…" Marigold hesitated and took a sideways glance at the monster, "…beast, is dead."

Cheers erupted from the crowd. A mass of noise, from which no individual could be heard.

"The four of us took the monster on," he continued. "For two nights we battled the creature, chasing it through hills and woods and plains." He was exaggerating, but it wasn't to make him and his men look better, no, it was to give the people a sense of satisfaction. Surely they would have been most disappointed to hear that the sun had barely moved in the sky from the drawing of Marigold's blade to its sheathing. "We lost no men, for we are seasoned at such sport, and we bring you the head of the… the White Gargunnoch… as proof." The words were salty in his mouth. "We come for our payment, and perhaps a place to eat, drink, and spend the night. Who speaks for you? Let him come forward."

A woman dressed in black pushed through the crowd. Young, ivory-skinned, black-haired, and with a voluptuous figure that Marigold couldn't help but take note of several times. "I speak for Hvitstein," she cried out in a tiny voice.

The city of Hvitstein really was not what Marigold was expecting.

"We have your goats, all one thousand of them," the woman shouted. "We have food for the feasting, wine and ale for the drinking, and music and women for the enjoying."

Marigold raised an eyebrow and looked at each of his men in turn. Haggar, despite his lifetime of debauchery, had turned a deep crimson. Evidently, that was not what *he* had been expecting either.

"Or men, if you prefer," she said with a wry smile, winking at Haggar with her dark eyes.

"Where is Dahl? Where is the man that gave us the contract? There are some words I'd like to have with him."

"Mr. Dahl has not yet returned from his travels. He has many places to visit. Will you eat and drink with us?"

How many more beasts had Hvitstein summoned? Were there other warriors out there taking down the easiest mark they ever had? Marigold took a moment to study the crowd. They all looked innocent enough, but there was obviously something amiss here. Even so, he wasn't going to just up and leave while he still might have those goats. Even if witchcraft was at work here, goatless farmers were likely to be more of a headache if he returned to them empty-handed. "We shall."

"Excellent. I am Adia, your host while you stay among us. Saddle your beasts at the stable and join us at the tavern in the centre of the city. The White Tower, you can't miss it. The festivities will last till sunrise." She began to retreat into the mass of colour behind her. "Leave the head of our friend right there. Let its blood soak into the grounds of our fair city. The Watch will hoist it up for all to see this evening. You may leave your weapons at the gates." She motioned to a number of men, and the pretty little thing was gone.

The rukhs were led away, and the men's weapons stacked against the wall of the gate tower. Marigold demanded that the door to the building remain open, and was met only with a nod and a grin from the hatted buffoon that stood inside. After a few moments, the crowd also began to withdraw. It almost appeared that they reversed away from the street, disappearing into the terraced housing. Within moments, not a man, woman, or child was in sight. The cheering and whooping was gone, giving way to a wind that slipped in and out of the numerous alleys with a howl.

Marigold stared down the brown length of packed dirt that ran through the middle of the town. "It's too fucking clean."

"Chief?" Sieg and Vik asked in unison.

"Too clean. Look how many of them there were. Hundreds of the bastards here, and not a cart of rubbish or pile of animal shit anywhere to be seen."

"S'a city, boss," said Vik. "Sure they take much better care of their home when they can't just up and move like we can."

"Vik, if there isn't some dark plot at work here, I'll eat my fucking helm, I promise you."

Vik laughed. "Come off it, Chief, you don't have a helm."

"No, I don't," Marigold answered. "And I won't bloody need one."

"Food's good, Chief. Eat a fucking scrap, will ya?" Vik tore into his leg of goat, holding the vast hunk of meat by a thick bone that protruded from the centre. "It's good, so, so good."

Juices and shreds of brown meat clung to Vik's beard. It was quite off-putting in truth, but that wasn't why Marigold had chosen not to eat. He eyed the crowd that filled the noisy tavern with mistrust. He and his crew were the only men present. The hall was filled with women. It was a pleasant view, but a pleasant view didn't mean that all was pleasant. The crowd that had welcomed them into Hvitstein had been an even mixture of both sexes. Where were the men now? Vik had wandered off for more meat, swinging a cup as he went and slopping ale over the women that milled about him. One of the women squealed with laughter as the liquid drenched her front. She tore off her top, chest bared to the room. Vik took note of this new development and showered the rest of the women around him with his drink. Clothes flew up and about the big man. He grinned back at Marigold.

"Nice tits, Chief, eh?" commented Sieg, emerging from a tankard the size of his head.

"I'll not disagree, but surely you can see there's something not right about this bloody place?"

"P'raps it's just their way of celebrating? Everyone does things their own way. Can you imagine what these folks would think if they saw us celebrating?"

"Right now, I think they'd believe us quite tame," he groaned as another young woman emerged from beneath Vik's legs. Two other buxom examples pushed their bodies into Vik's back and dragged him off to the end of the hall.

"Well, what are we waiting for?" laughed Sieg.

"Sieg," warned Marigold, "save for Haggar, we've all women waiting for us at home."

"I don't think they're watching, Marigold."

"They don't fucking need to be. Let one of those women anywhere near your cock and stones and no matter how much you scrub them before you're home, it's the first thing your woman'll ask you about. Mark my bloody words, it's some Pit-granted ability they have."

"Caught out before, eh, Chief? Well, fuck it. I'm going to risk it," Sieg grinned. "Haggar!"

Haggar turned from the table he was sat at, chewing vigorously, eyes wide at the sights he was seeing.

"Shall we join in? Don't want to miss out on this!"

Marigold watched as Haggar smiled and got up to join Sieg. The two men slapped each other across their shoulders and delved into the crowd. Within moments the horde was upon them, whooping and crying out with a primal delight that Marigold did not expect to hear from a civilised city. Unclothed flesh bounced this way and that, the dim light blanketing all but the flailing limbs in shadow. Marigold was sure it was fun out there in the middle of it, but from here it looked like some writhing, demonic nightmare. As he turned his back to his near-drained cup, he found a familiar face sat on the bench next to him, her body draped in thin, black silk that left nothing to the imagination.

"Adia," Marigold greeted.

"I don't believe we've really had the chance to talk, Marigold," she slurred, gesturing with a cup that was clearly not her first of the evening.

"Wasn't really expecting to talk," said Marigold. "Brought you the head of the beast. We just want our payment and we'll be away. There's work to be done back home."

"Well that's very cold, Marigold. It looks like everyone but you is having fun." She reached out with her free hand, winding a lock of Marigold's yellow hair around a finger. "Don't you want some fun too?" She tightened her grip and pulled Marigold's head close to hers. "You're far from home," she whispered. "Far from home and among new friends. We really should get to know each other a little better." Adia rolled her head back, exposing the pure white skin of her neck and chest. Only narrow strips of fabric covered the essentials. She ran her tongue slowly around her lips and laughed.

"Fuck this," Marigold spat, wrenching his hair back from her and spilling the remainder of her liquor. Hurriedly, he got up from the bench and pushed past the edge of the crowd, kicking the door to the tavern wide open. It was good to be washed in cold, clean air, free from the stink of sweat and sex and drink.

The night was clear, the stars hung in the shining constellations overhead. Greldin's Axe gleamed clearly above. Marigold took one look at it and breathed out heavily through his nose. Who else was watching them tonight, aside from the Gods? He stalked away from the debauchery and made his way through the clean and straight streets of Hvitstein. At the halfway point between The White Tower and the closed drawbridge, he turned left, which marked the route to the stables that the rukhs had been put up in. As he approached the lantern-lit front of the wooden structure, a squawk from the one of the rukhs was followed by the pained cry of a man and a burst of straw into the street. Marigold ran to the scene to find an ancient fellow clutching a bloodied shoulder, and Sieg's ruffled rukh, Sofia, stomping its stout, yellow feet violently into the dirt. Its enormous beak opened to screech once more, and only then did Marigold understand what else it was that he was seeing. The other three rukhs lay in the straw, bleeding from wounds to the neck. Dead. The man, still reeling from his attack, clutched a long and curved blade that was pointed at Sieg's rukh. Marigold glared at the elderly prick, whose head darted back and forth between barbarian and bird. His eyes were white with fear, his toothless gums trembled in his open mouth.

Marigold balled up a fist and hurled it into the bastard's face. The fellow crumpled in a heap below the last living rukh, and was immediately set upon by it. Lucky fucker got away without feeling much of that. The bloody-beaked beast nuzzled its head against Marigold as he bent down to retrieve the fallen blade.

"Good work. Too bad we'll have to fucking walk home now, though."

What else was Hvitstein really up to tonight? The orgy. Marigold left the stable and ran full pelt back to the tavern. It was all too obvious. It wasn't always good to be right. The promiscuity should have told him all he fucking needed. City-women don't just lather themselves all over men like him. Shit, in his earlier days he had tried several times, and earned nothing more than a slap to the face or a kick to the stones. Or both.

Marigold kicked the door to the tavern in and the wave of rancid heat hit him once again. He stumbled at the sight. The whole fucking place was heaving with ancient, haggard crones. Naked, wrinkled bodies sagged in all corners. All of them crawling over one another to paw at the seated figures of three men that were bound to their chairs at the back of the room.

"Vik, Sieg, Haggar, you weak-willed trio of fucking cunts! Get up, we're bloody done here," he roared.

A cacophony of titters and cackles filled the low-ceilinged inn as the hags closest to him prostrated themselves, reaching out their skinny and dark-veined hands.

"Join us," they moaned in unison.

Marigold looked back at his men. A glistening and red curtain below their necks told the story. A glint of steel beneath Haggar's chin named the method.

"We were promised one final night to be young, and we were promised you," came a dusty voice from behind.

Marigold spun to find a woman with liver-spotted skin, sagging eyelids, and fleshy jowls. She wobbled as she swayed in the doorway. The clinging black silk marked her out as Adia, but an Adia that had to have been a hundred winters older than the one he had met before. "What cursed witchcraft is this, hag? What did you do to my men?"

The old woman laughed, her body wracked with spasms it could barely withstand. "Their souls left them at the peak of excitement, Marigold. Such unearthly pleasures are not found elsewhere, not this side of the Pits. Join them! Revel! Delight!"

"I'll have your heads on the end of a fucking pike, woman!"

Adia waved her hand across her face, revealing her young figure again as it passed. "Cezare gave us this night to enjoy. There won't be another for us without your blood. Girls!"

Marigold felt hands and nails across his shoulders and back, clinging on, trying to pull him down. Lucky for him it was a bunch of lithe women that weighed next to nothing. Marigold threw several of them over his head together, sending them careening into Adia where they all collapsed in a heap at the doorway. "That Pit-spawned, cock-loving, cunt of a wizard," he raged. "Why the fuck has he sent us all the way out-" That was also too obvious, now that he really thought about it.

Cezare's days in that tower of his were numbered.

Marigold glared at the women strewn about him and saw only death. His fists swung this way and that. Blood spurted, screams ripped the air, lanterns swung violently to and fro. Bones crunched beneath Marigold's feet, skin tore beneath his fingers, noses burst behind his knuckles. The room became the very vision of the Pits that no doubt spawned this cursed magic in the first place. Adia's head emerged from within the tangle of broken women, eyes wild, lips flapping unknown curses that were directed at Marigold.

Marigold launched a blood-caked chair at her, embedding a leg in the middle of her once desirable face. The supple skin that bled around it returned to that of the ancient being she really was, her gnarled, pointing finger fell limp and her reaching arm slumped down.

A string of expletives spewed from Marigold as he picked his way across the dying and the dead. Cezare. Fucking Cezare! How could he have been so stupid to have come this far without realising that that particular wand-twiddling prick was behind everything? A wizard on his turf, stolen goats, a contract offering goats in distant lands, and a settlement left without a leader? Marigold was a fucking idiot, and he knew it. Out of Illis, out of the way. Cezare free to do what he pleased. No good ever came from allowing a wizard quarter in your lands. No good ever came from letting a wizard breathe, for that matter. He ran back for Sieg's rukh and charged with her to the drawbridge. Without hesitation, he slew the sleeping fellow by the chain and winch of the gatehouse and grabbed his sword. The drawbridge was dropped with a crash. He slung Sear over his shoulders and leapt back onto the bird. He beat her flanks viciously as the pair started the long ride home.

Marigold's heart pounded. It beat even faster than the taloned feet of the rukh beneath his legs. Elvi. She was going to be safe. She had to be safe. There were plenty of warriors left at the camp, and she was no stranger to an axe herself. Vik, Sieg, and Haggar... Well, he had a long time to dwell upon how he had failed them.

Chapter Six

UNDERDOG

These stairwells could have done with something more than grey stone and the odd torch. They really were becoming quite tedious. Each of them wound upwards in exactly the same way. Same width, same height, same colour. Nonetheless, even with their uniform design, Marigold still managed to catch his foot on one of the final stones, pitching himself chest first onto the uneven flagstones of the sixth floor of Cezare's funhouse.

He took a moment to get the breath back into his lungs, and quickly became very aware of something watching him. He looked up to see the bottom of several pillars and a pair of pale green calves fitted into steel boots. The calves – the most interesting, and potentially dangerous thing he had noted – became knees, became a mail tunic, became the seated form of an aged and one-eyed roughskin, or 'gretch' as the beasts referred to themselves as. A roughskin was a lot like a man, except for the notable negatives of them not dying quite as easily, having flat noses that were no good for breaking, and impressively protruding lower jaws, held in place by oversized, sharp teeth that gave them quite the underbite. Roughskins spoke the common tongue, but their dentally challenged maws mangled it somewhat. That probably explained why they hated the name 'roughskin'; 'gretch' was at least something they could manage.

Marigold picked himself up and brushed off the dust. He readjusted Sear behind his back. Quite the embarrassing entrance. The eye-patched roughskin sat before him had to be the oldest specimen he had ever seen. They were strong beasts, but were so prone to brutal in-fighting that few of them managed to live to see their few wispy strands of hair grow grey. This one looked particularly bored, probably hadn't had a fight in hours. "Bit fucking dramatic, don't you think? Just sat there like that, waiting?" he asked the aged roughskin. "How long have you been sat there? If you've been waiting for me this whole time your arse'll be as numb as the stone you're sat on."

The roughskin shifted in its seat, perhaps accepting Marigold's concern about circulation.

"Don't talk much, eh? Well, fine by me. Means we can get to it faster." Marigold made for Sear's hilt.

"You're done, Marigold, your time hash come to an end," the roughskin snarled.

"Well, now, that sounds quite like you know me."

"Korag knowsh Marigold, and Marigold knowsh Korag. Fink back, warrior."

"Korag? Hmm… Korag," Marigold pondered, tapping his foot and rubbing his chin. "The missing eye?" Marigold nodded towards Korag's eyepatch. "Was, er… Was that me?"

Korag's face crumpled with disappointment. "Yesh."

Marigold chewed over that tidbit of information for a moment. Yes. He did vaguely remember a Korag. "Korag! You see, that's why I didn't recognise you. The eyepatch is new, isn't it? Well, it's part of why I didn't recognise you; it's been about twenty fucking winters since we fought, you halfwit, and you're not the only roughskin I've dealt with since then."

"Sho confident. Shtill sho shmug."

"I beg your pardon?"

"We'll fight, Marigold. Vish'll be the lasht fight you begin," Korag mocked. The eye-patched roughskin yanked on a slender chain that hung by his stone seat. It triggered a grinding that began to sound from within the stone walls of the room. Six doors began to open; the join between wall and door was hardly visible. A younger roughskin had been waiting behind each, and all six strode smugly into the room, forming a loose circle around the pair. "You shee, even if you besht me, my children will tear you to shredsh."

"They've been waiting in these bloody walls as long as you've been sat there, haven't they?" Marigold laughed incredulously. He forced himself not to swallow. A mix of excitement and a twinge of uncertainty had him by the throat. It wasn't the first time that he had faced overwhelming odds, and if he could help it, it wasn't going to be the last time either. Seven on one. The rush, the thrill, the fear of knowing that each breath could be the last. He only had himself to rely on, and that was just the way he liked it.

The six newcomers, in varying shades of green, were all kitted out in basic armour and held a mixture of weapons; sickles and whips, axes and daggers. They stood in still silence, awaiting Korag's word.

"Sho, Marigold, who shtrikesh firsht?" Korag's leg was jiggling below his seat impatiently. Twenty years was a long time to await revenge, or, in Marigold's opinion, a long time to entertain the idea that it might actually happen.

"Look, I'm sure the kids you and your mother had together are very strong and capable, but you're forgetting one thing: I haven't dealt with that cunt on the top floor yet, and nothing is going to stop me painting my jerkin red with his blood."

"Korag prepared to give Marigold firsht attack. Shonsh not move until Korag shay."

"Korag's done very well," Marigold mocked. "Korag will be training dogs next."

"Enough!" Korag yelled, and stamped his foot on the stone.

The circle tightened. The young roughskins loped towards Marigold. There wasn't enough time to pull Sear out now, and certainly not enough to get her flaming. This was going to hurt.

"Tell you what, Korag, I'm going to say that none of this counts unless you," he jabbed a finger directly at the seated roughskin, "make the final blow."

And with that, a collection of green knuckles and fists rained their attacks upon Marigold.

Into the ribs.

"Fuck," he wheezed.

Into the back.

"Fuck!" he spat.

One lamped him in the side of the head.

"Bastards!" he yelled.

Twelve fists from everywhere at once. Marigold found himself slipping down onto one knee, weathering the blows but unable to block a single one. Marigold's layer of muscle was thick – thicker than most men could dream of – but it wasn't armour, and it was all he could do to keep it clenched. When his mind told him to stop one punch from the left, a smash from the right knocked the thought clean out. Within moments that felt like an age, Marigold was on both knees. A fist caught him in the centre of the cheek. He bit his tongue, felt a second tooth wobble. Stars danced in his vision, what he could see began to blur. Was that a headache pounding, or was it actually just a fist? Throughout the beating, Marigold caught flashes of Korag. The bastard remained sat, hacking out a throaty laugh, slapping his thigh in delight, dangling strings of white drool beneath his underbite.

Then, a long and hairy arm began to wind itself around Marigold's neck. As the limb tightened, Marigold felt strong hands hold him in place. A metal boot touched down on his back. There was no point even trying to struggle now. What had that been about overwhelming odds?

"Have hish eye out, ladsh. Make vish a fair fight."

"Fucking fair?" Marigold gurgled. "I've taken a beating *and* you want my eye out? You've had twenty damned years to heal, you prick."

"Eye not grow back. Fair."

He had the beginnings of a point.

The headlock somehow became even tighter, and Marigold became dimly aware of a young roughskin face directly before him. The crouched fucker cocked his head to one side and cracked a nightmarish grin. Hot and rancid breath burned Marigold's eyes, but it was with a grim understanding that he accepted that would only affect one of them for a moment longer anyway. The roughskin before him reached out a thick finger. It was the most hideous finger that he had ever seen his life, now that he came to think about it. Long and green, with wide knuckles that were probably larger than his eye socket, and sporting a nail that was unlikely to have been called clean in its whole life on the end of that gross digit. Finger laughed, revelling in the moment, drawing it all out and giving Marigold ample time to consider the situation that was heading his way.

"Fuck," Marigold seethed between his clamped jaws. A fucking eye. And it was hardly going to be removed with any form of surgical precision by this bastard. This was going to ruin his swordsmanship further down the line, and he could forget about ever firing a bow again.

A familiar, tittering cackle crept into the room, from the stairs behind Marigold and the five pricks holding him down. He felt the pressure around his neck slacken as the one that had him in the headlock reared up to see what the noise was all about. The fingers that gripped him relaxed, and the boot left his back entirely as shrill laughter bloomed around the room.

Very *familiar* laughter.

Tiny feet touched down on Marigold's bruised spine and ran along his vertebrae, over Sear, onto his neck. A clawed foot dug in to his scalp before it leapt off. A red creature lunged directly for the face of Finger. It was one of those little imp bastards from the floor below.

"Thank Greldin's fucking axe for my incompetence," Marigold chuckled, as several more of the demonic beings appeared and leapt for the faces of the roughskins, like tiny, savage dogs.

Korag's face dropped. Glee became utter dismay within the space of a heartbeat. Marigold tore his arms free of the remaining roughskins – who were all too busy trying to save their own eyes now – and closed the space between himself and Korag.

"Jusht you an-"

Before Korag could finish his sentence, Marigold thrust his own strong forefinger deep into the last remaining eyeball of the ancient roughskin leader. It triggered a brief memory of doing exactly the same, long ago, albeit on the other side of Korag's face. Nerves and sinew twanged against his nail. The tip touched bone. White juices tinged with swirls of red cascaded out over Marigold's second knuckle. Too bad for Marigold that

Korag's brain was too small and too far back in the green-skinned fool's thick skull for even his long fingers to reach.

Korag spent a horrific moment in profound silence. His mouth agape, his brow raised as high as it could go, as if he was at least *trying* to stare in stunned amazement. Marigold removed his finger with a squelch as air rushed into the newly formed cavity. Blood poured from the wound. Korag's hands shot out like lightning, reaching for Marigold's face. The barbarian was too slow to react, and the roughskin gripped the sides of Marigold's head tightly, one sharp-nailed hand firmly clasped over his left ear. The long thumbs of Korag searched blindly, flicking this way and that, desperate to find eye sockets of their own to delve into. Marigold kicked hard at Korag, but the enraged beast lurched from his seat and toppled into Marigold. The pair crashed to the floor. Blood and eye fluids slopped over Marigold's face, into his eyes, into his mouth. As the old warriors grappled one another on the floor, one of Korag's sons tottered backwards and tripped over his father, imp still scratching away at him. Korag tumbled over with him, still clinging to Marigold's head. Marigold felt searing pain only for a second as his ear was torn clean off, held fast in the grip of Korag.

Well, it was a markedly better result than the eye scenario.

Korag wasted not a moment and cupped his massive hand with Marigold's lost ear to his mouth. It was somewhat sickening for the barbarian to see a blind monster chew furiously on a piece of his own body, but it created enough of a delay for Marigold to roll out of the way, into a space in the room that wasn't occupied with a roughskin and imp combo. Marigold gingerly ran his fingers over the wound. There was a lot of blood, and his head felt weird as the sounds of fighting rushed passed the flat hole in the side of his head. He gave himself a moment to survey the chaotic situation. The roughskins had all but dealt with the intruders, the ones that had freed themselves began helping their stricken brothers. Either these imps were a lot more competent than the ones Marigold had smushed together earlier, or these young roughskins hadn't been trained at all in dealing with surprises.

Too bad they weren't going to get another chance to do so if it was the latter.

Marigold finally unsheathed Sear.

Korag was back on his feet, screaming at the top of his lungs and thrashing his limbs in all directions, lost in an abyss that was never going to clear. A literal blind rage. One of the roughskins lay gibbering on the floor with its throat torn out and a dead, bloody-mouthed imp clutched in its hand. Two of the other roughskins were helping a third rid itself of the imp that was tearing into its head. The remaining two were grappling for weapons from the scattered mess, their eyes fixed firmly on Marigold. One of them picked up an axe, the other one reached for a chain whip. Marigold recognised that particular fucker as Finger.

The two sides charged into each other.

Finger and Axe began a pincer attack. Finger snapped his whip into the space behind him and cracked it across the room with surprising accuracy. The chain spike on the end wrapped itself around Marigold's thick forearm. Veins pushed up to the surface of his tanned flesh as he yanked Finger towards him, knocking him off balance and sending him tripping neck first into Sear's eagerly awaiting tip. As Finger fell from the blade, Axe ran faster, snarling with his weapon held aloft. Marigold swung Sear with the whip still wrapped around his arm and sheared Axe's head clean off.

Korag twisted on the spot, arms grasping at air. "What'sh happening? Boysh?"

Imphead and his brothers had dealt with their problem, and the trio swung heads over shoulders to face what they had obviously deemed to be the lesser of the threats in the room. Big mistake. That threat was now storming his way towards them, dragging his impromptu whip bracelet behind him. Marigold gripped Sear tightly in his right hand as he smashed it deep into the solar plexus of the brother to the left. His other fist struck upwards, into the jaw of the brother on the right. Shards of tooth burst forth from the shattered jaw. Both roughskins crumpled to the deck. Marigold swiped Sear across the throats of both.

From beside a pillar on the far side of the circular room, Korag stretched his gaping, empty eye sockets.

Imphead began backing further away. He waved his green palms frantically in a plea for mercy. Marigold jerked his arm and collected a length of the whip that trailed behind him. Imphead's attempt to bat Marigold away was as pathetic as the guard that had donated his limbs at the beginning of this venture. He expected more of roughskins. Marigold wound the whip around Imphead's throat and tugged hard. The coward's green face darkened, reddening slightly in the cheeks. Eyes bulged, mouth wheezed, desperately trying to suck air into a flattened windpipe. Blood was forced out from the labyrinth of gashes the imp had made on his bald head. Marigold ground his teeth together as he stared, mad-eyed, into the ebbing face of the last of the young roughskins. Fuck, his earhole hurt.

Korag breathed in sharply, twisting this way and that, desperate for even an idea of how the fight was going.

Marigold dumped Imphead's lifeless body to the flagstones. A dagger clattered as it fell from his lifeless hands. The only sounds remaining were Marigold's panting and Korag's wails. There wasn't as much blood as there had been downstairs, but it still wasn't a pretty sight. Marigold found himself hoping that Cezare had paid the group in advance, and that the green bastards had at least had a chance to enjoy their last payment. Korag, despite his grievous wounds, seemed to cotton on to the general lack of the movement in the room.

"Shonsh?" he called out, "Ish he dead? Ish Marigold dead?"

Marigold left the silence to hang for a moment.

"Marigold?"

"You've lost. Again."

"Korag'sh children?"

"Dead, damn you. You sentenced your entire family to death when you made them fight me!"

It was Korag that remained silent now.

Marigold smeared the blood drenching Sear across Imphead's corpse before sheathing her. He checked himself over, carefully running his fingers over the forest of welts that had joined the gashes from the previous floor. There was nothing he could do about the ear. The old prick had swallowed it, and even if he hadn't, Marigold was no seamstress. He was just going to have to listen very carefully with his remaining ear from now on. The loss would have been easier to take if he still had his wife, it might even have made his life simpler.

It was time to move on up to the next floor, there was nothing left for him on this one, and there couldn't be much more of this madhouse left to climb now.

"Marigold," Korag said quietly from the far side of the room.

"What, Korag?"

"Finish Korag. Don't leave Korag to feshter."

Marigold paced across the room, careful to tread around Korag in case there was a ruse at work deep inside Korag's addled mind. After all, the bastard had been waiting twenty years for this moment, failed though it was. He sat down upon the stone throne in the middle of the room and plucked a roughskin-made dagger from the flagstones by it. Shit, the seat really was uncomfortable, though the bruises on his arse were probably playing a big part in that. The dagger he examined wasn't quite as good as the clan-made one he still had in his boot.

"Here," Marigold shouted, throwing the dagger over to Korag's feet. "Sort yourself out."

Korag swung about, angling his head to try and work out where the weapon fell. "Marigold!" he pleaded, "Kill me. I've losht everyfing. Let me die a warriorsh deff."

"So have I, Korag. I've lost it all. And you know what? We've only our Pit-cursed fucking selves to blame for any of it."

Marigold slowly rose from the stone. He stretched, pulling all of the bruises and knotted muscles out before they began to seize up. There was still work to be done, and more than likely the worst of it was yet to come.

Chapter Seven

NADIR

"What the fuck is this?" Marigold growled as he left the stairs, bewildered with the sight that greeted him.

The room was somehow much wider than the one below, which obviously wasn't possible in a tower that tapered as it rose. On the far side of this dark and pillared floor stood a grand, wooden door. A door that was barred shut with an arm and a fucking leg. Between Marigold and the door lay the body that was missing the arm and the leg. The body that Marigold knew – just damn well knew – lay in the same spot right at the bottom of this tower. The ceiling was high and vaulted again, not like the flat ceilings of the floors above the foyer. That bloody green moss was creeping out between the cracks, and the space even felt and smelt damp. A dull rumbling and squawking beyond the door sounded like the rukh was just beyond, pecking people to shreds.

"By Greldin, not this shit again." His hand shot to the back of his neck, groping around for some new leech latched onto his neck, sucking his blood and feeding him dreams. Instead, he found the old, circular set of puncture wounds but no fleshy mass above them to crush. He turned to head back down the steps. Maybe going back down and up again would yield different results.

The winding staircase was gone. Flat flags paved the floor all around Marigold, hints of green moss and weeds decorated the damp edges.

"Cezare! I've had just about enough of your bloody magic," he roared. "Grow some stones and get down here. Fight me like a man, you insufferable bitch."

It was a shitty trick. Another attempt to pull the wool over Marigold's eyes. Cezare might have a low opinion of his guest's intellect, but Marigold was quite certain that this was not the ground floor. For a start, the illusion hadn't included a set of steps upwards. A sealed floor, then. Something cerebral to work out. Again. Just what he needed after taking a brutal fucking pounding to the head.

Marigold walked gingerly into the middle of the room; a laughable sight. He didn't want to say that he was scared of what might be brewing in this room – there was very little that did scare him – but he was certainly wary. He held one open palm close to his throat – in case of more summoned hands – and one close to the hilt of Sear. The muscles in his arms rippled and flexed, eager for something to show itself and bring some kind of reality to the situation. This was rukh shit. All of it, a slopping pile of stinking rukh shit.

Marigold stood over the mutilated corpse with the snapped neck that he had left to rot at the beginning of this venture. The pool of blood that had flowed from each of the severed limbs had congealed into a dark and sticky mess, and was slick enough that Marigold was able to catch the vague reflection of himself in it. He toed the body with his boot. The whole thing moved together, stiff with death. The man's torn face – set at a sickening angle – was a lot paler now that the body had time to drain itself over the stones. Glazed eyes stared off in different directions, and the fellow's pink tongue hung out of his gaping mouth, cracked and dry.

Utterly dead.

"Not going to reanimate him for me, then?" Marigold called out. His words bounced around the room, and that was the only answer he got.

The barbarian took a deep breath and strode to the door. He didn't like this at all. Cezare was clearly one of those fuckers that dabbled in a variety of magics. Summoning, illusion, blood, possibly mind control. Marigold was forced to admit to himself that the cunt was rather good at it, too. The severed arm and the leg that held the door tightly shut were both completely rigid. It appeared that limbs really could make fine replacements for planks. Yanking the body parts out from between the handles was harder work than it had been shoving them in, but eventually the two pieces came away as three. Marigold clasped his great hands around the brass handles and jerked them towards himself. A burst of red sun directly ahead dazzled him. He rubbed his eyes as the doors continued their inward journey, squinted through the light to see exactly what he had expected: Illis, from about seven floors higher than he was used to seeing it.

This was most certainly not the ground floor.

From high up here, the trees seemed like tiny bushes, the roads like yellow scratches between the patchwork of goatless fields. The charred blot of land that used to be his camp still smouldered. Everything was bathed in the warm glow of the setting sun. It might have been a pleasant view if Marigold had had time for such fancies. He peered carefully over the edge, keeping his feet planted firmly on the stone within the threshold. Some fucking drop that was. Did Cezare actually expect him to just give up, open up, and walk straight out? Marigold barked a laugh. Cezare really had a lot to learn about Marigold.

And then he was airborne.

Too late did Marigold feel the shove; the welts and gashes masking the extra pressure. Still, whoever did it was not the chief concern on the warrior's mind at this point. The cut-stone lip of the hole in the side of the tower fled upwards as the sky twisted beneath him. Up became the dirt and grass far below. Marigold, solid and heavy enough that the jolt hadn't pushed him too far outwards, threw out desperate fingers on a quest for purchase.

The fall ended almost as quickly as it had begun, thank Greldin, though Marigold would have preferred it to have not happened at all. The weight of Sear pulling down on his back was not welcome. His fingers gripped tightly to a mere sliver of a groove in the stone of the tower's side. It wasn't the first time he had found himself dangling over a precipice, and with his shitty luck it probably wasn't going to be the last. Marigold's fingertips had become remarkably strong and agile over the years, able to seek out the tiniest of cracks and meagre fingerholds in short order. But as brave and as fearless as he was, even he couldn't be ashamed of the pulse he felt pounding in his neck. If it didn't simmer down it was going to damn well knock him off altogether.

"Oh for fuck's sake," whined a nasal voice from above.

Marigold slowly creaked his head upwards. Cezare? No. But it was a weasel-faced arsehole that he had hoped to be able to deal with at some point.

"Not even intelligent enough to just fall to your death, are you? Have to drag it out. Well, what are you going to do? Stay clinging there for the rest of your life like some barbaric spider? Just get on with it and let go. Cezare isn't going to be pleased about this, he isn't going to be pleased at all."

"Dahl, you inbred, hag-loving cock!" Marigold panted from his perch on the side of the tower. "How I've wanted the chance to bump into you again."

"Well, aha, we certainly had a little bump, didn't we? Pity for you I'm just out of reach, eh?"

Marigold would soon fucking see about that. He clenched tightly with one hand and stretched up with another. Fingers crept across the stone, digging into the barest of holds and pushing down with a force that held just firmly enough for him to repeat the actions. With painstakingly slow progress, Marigold closed the gap between himself, the threshold, and the snake that got him into this mess. Veins bulged in his arms, sweat glistened and ran between the grooves of his muscles in rivulets. He gritted his teeth and watched as that odious prick above began pacing back and forth across the entrance, notably panicked by this unexpected turn of events.

"You're going... to answer..." Marigold grumbled through gritted teeth as he ascended, "for sending me... to Hvitstein. And maybe... you'll learn... what a fucking gargunnoch is."

"Oh, yes," said Dahl with dismay. "I-I couldn't find a gargunnoch, but that great white brute I summoned certainly did the job of getting you there anyway, whatever it was. Summoned it myself, you know?" he said proudly. "Cezare taught me how to do it, and he'll be teaching me more once I've held up my end of this bargain. Oh, and that is offing you and harvesting your blood, in case you were wondering." Dahl clutched his hips with his hands and looked out towards the setting sun. "I'll be quite the force, Marigold. I'll have nothing to fear when I can summon any creature suitable to do my bidding."

The weasel had become too wrapped up in his own delusions of grandeur to realise that Marigold was mere inches from safety. Fingers from the enraged barbarian wrapped themselves around Dahl's ankle.

"No, no, no, no no!" he panicked, trying to look in every direction at once for some way out his imminent predicament.

A vicious grin split Marigold's face, despite his own dire situation.

"No! No! Nnn... Nnn!" Begging fast became wailing, as expected. The cries of the guilty and the damned. Peals of despair as the fellow began to realise that his wrongdoings weren't going to lengthen his existence in the manner he had expected them to. "G-get off, dog!"

Some last ditch attempt that was.

Marigold tugged.

Even in his doom, the little man still tried to save himself, pitching headfirst into Marigold and wedging himself between the hilt of Sear and the warrior's shredded back. He managed to wrap his cold, stringy fingers around Marigold's neck. There wasn't enough power behind them to give Marigold any breathing difficulties, but there was enough in the grip for Dahl to temporarily delay his all but certain death.

"I'll kill us both! We'll both fall, Marigold," Dahl babbled. "Climb back up! Now! I'll do it!"

"Do what? I've had midges that were more troublesome than you," Marigold answered irritably as he continued his slow ascent. He wriggled to shift the crawling summoner from his back, but Dahl so was light that he couldn't unbalance him. The edge of the doorway was so close, just out of reach. Marigold threw his free arm about, trying to rid himself from the fucking tagnut that was scrabbling around so desperately.

"Stop it, stop it, stop it!" the man screamed into Marigold's ruined lughole. "You'll kill me! No! Don't kill me!"

"Killing you is the pissing plan, so get fucking used to it!" Marigold retaliated, slipping in his rage. He gripped the wall as tightly as the thin cracks within it would allow. Fingernails threatened to tear right off as he dug in, but the drop loosened the parasite. Marigold dared to take one hand from the wall and grabbed Dahl's spindly leg. As he clutched desperately to his stone lifeline with one hand, he yanked at the limb. Fingers clawed at Marigold's head in panic, a digit scraped across the open hole that was once his ear. Amidst bellows of pain and thrashing about, Marigold finally held Dahl out in the open, over the sickening drop to the world below. The bulbous gold necklace that the weasel had worn so proudly at their first meeting slipped from around his neck and plummeted to the earth. Marigold gave Dahl a moment to trace its fall. "Summon your way out of this, you well-dressed prick," he spat, and let go.

Well, Dahl certainly tried his best to do something to escape the fate that rushed to meet him. His arms and legs flailed. Unfamiliar words screeched in terror ripped through the air. The figure became smaller and smaller, and that was the end of Dahl. Unless, of course, the fool had actually summoned himself a red cloud to land on. Seemed doubtful.

"Good riddance," Marigold spat, and watched the blob of saliva as it whirled through the air.

The weary warrior flung an arm over the edge of the doorway and hauled himself up into it. He pushed himself onto his knees and rested there, panting heavily. He wiped a smear of sweat and blood from his forehead and observed the room around him.

It was different.

Empty. Pillars, a flat ceiling, slit windows. There were no mosses or weeds growing between the stones of the floor. No body adorned the centre. Dry. It appeared smaller now; the correct size. Marigold twisted his aching neck to look over his shoulder. A solid stone wall. No door in it. What in the Pits had he just climbed through?

It occurred to Marigold that all that had just transpired may not have actually taken place. That prick Dahl might still be alive somewhere. Marigold was a man that could rip a head from shoulders. He was a man that could take down a hulking gargunnoch alone. He was a man that could face seven fucking roughskins and come out breathing on the other side. He was not a man that could deal with a tower that changed its form around him. Much better to simply get to the source of the witchcraft, ensure that it was dismantled into as many parts as possible, and bother himself with the matter no more. Still, there was a most welcome addition to this new rendition of the shape-shifting seventh floor; twirling stairs upwards, the likes of which he knew all too well. Marigold readjusted the strap holding Sear to his back and pulled his crumpled jerkin down as he trotted towards them. He'd rather not face the wizard with his fucking stones dangling in plain sight.

Chapter Eight

THE SECOND GOODBYE

"What in the damn Pits is this, Cezare?" Marigold demanded as he arrived on floor eight.

This space, unlike all others before it, was adorned with white, silken sheets that were fastened to the walls between the windows. The fabric cascaded down to the floor and spread across the stone tiles underfoot. Any grey visible between the material was peppered with red petals. A huge, white-sheeted, wrought-iron bed sat at the far end. Weird. Marigold was becoming quite sick of weird surprises. He came here to fight, not think.

"I'm flattered at the sentiment. A nice rest before I head on up and tear you apart? But really? I'd prefer a leg of meat and a horn of ale."

Something stirred from behind the bed. Marigold lurched forward, fingers flexing, ready to tear apart whatever monstrosity was lying in wait.

A bare foot and slender calf slid out, followed by a fine figure of a thigh. The leg was joined by a tall, female body dressed in a sheer, white gown. A body shaped just the way Marigold liked it. Too much so. With a clipped breath, he traced the figure from toes to face. Marigold swallowed as he beheld a delicate chin and nose, framed by long, raven locks that hung in thick braids over a familiar chest.

Marigold swallowed. "Elvi?" his voice cracked. It couldn't be?

The creature that looked a lot like his dead wife glided gracefully across the room. Her arms reached up as she neared Marigold. She draped them around him. He was too stunned to move. She smiled her perfect smile; a small scar over her lip dragged her face into that knowing sneer he loved so much. Her green eyes sparkled as he gazed into them. He found his hands reaching around her, running up her body. The body of a woman he was all too aware he had buried this day.

"You've shaved your head, my love," she said, running her fingers through the irregular clumps that decorated Marigold's scalp. "Didn't make a very good job of it, did you?"

"Aye, well it was quick. Didn't want no cunt grabbing it while I'm trying to fight."

"That's awful language, Marigold," she cocked her head to one side, eyes narrowed.

With difficulty, Marigold tore his gaze away from hers to stare at a black-cloaked figure that had appeared beyond her. A second figure out from behind this bloody bed. Clumps of long, dark hair hung from the shadowed cowl, just like on the second floor. Cezare! It fucking had to be! Marigold shook his head and let go of his dead wife. His fingers grasped for his blade, but the pale arms came back for him. "No!" He pushed against the woman. "You're all spells and no stones, Cezare," he shouted. "Hiding behind women now? Get over here and fucking face me." The cloaked presence recoiled.

The woman that somehow might have been Elvi shoved her smooth knee up into Marigold's crotch with a crunch. It wasn't the first time his stones had taken a blow from his wife, but this time had to be among the last of them. Marigold went down, just the same as anybody else would. He fought the sickness that rose in his throat, the pains that swelled in his stomach, the shaking that wracked his legs. With an effort, he rolled back up to his knees. He looked up at Elvi. Her foot slammed into his throat, just beneath his chin. Down he went again, gagging and spluttering, onto his front. Marigold attempted to crawl away from the woman on his elbows and knees. It couldn't be her. He spat a red mixture into the white cloth beneath and felt a weight lifted from his back. Sear had been dragged from her sheath. He waited, somewhat patiently, for her to shear through his neck. Should he bother breathing out? Say something clever? Instead heard the clatter of metal on stone as she was flung across the room. Elvi always had been a strong one, and this imposter seemed to be no bloody different in that regard. The dagger in his boot strap was taken next, cast to the other side of the room. Out of reach. A heel came down onto the middle of Marigold's back. His elbows splayed to the sides, his chin and chest took up their role. He rolled over onto his back, panting heavily. She was smiling at him.

"I almost bit my fucking tongue off, witch!"

"Oh, she's no witch," said Cezare, appearing at Elvi's side. So close. "She's just flesh and blood, like you and I."

"It's another of your clever fucking tricks is what it is! She ain't my shitting woman!" Pulses of agony from his crushed stones still reached deep into his body. He'd have preferred to have had the bastards cut off at this point. Cezare was right fucking there, and he was helpless. Pathetic.

Elvi smiled sweetly, stood between Marigold and Cezare.

"And why do you say that, my barbaric friend?"

"Are you fucking kidding? Why in Greldin's name do you think I'm here, you unhinged prick? I buried my wife this morning, in a proper fucking grave! I did that before I vowed to myself to end you on the same day."

"Well," Cezare said dismissively, as he played with his fingers, "you didn't bury all of her."

Marigold pushed air out through his teeth. Flecks of blood drifted out through the new space between them. Elvi's body hadn't been in the best state when he had found her. Nobody had been in one piece. But she had both arms, both legs. Her head had been nearby. It was more than he could have said for some of the poor bastards he had uncovered in the heaps.

"It doesn't take much, to bring a person back, you know?"

"Fuck you!"

"The Elvi you see here was nothing more than a nipple on my lectern, but I've studied hard, and I've studied well. She's good isn't she? I'd say she's damn near a perfect copy of her."

"It's not her."

"Well..." Cezare watched as Elvi sauntered over to the bed and spread herself onto it. Her long legs reached into the air over the twisted iron design at the end of the bed. "It is and it isn't."

"And what the fuck does that mean?"

"Her body is perfect. Down to the finest details. You'll not find a freckle you don't remember. Her mind? Well... You remember everything about her, and that's all that's really necessary. You want her back, correct? You want that smell, that figure, that lust she had for you. You know, Marigold, I've sampled the lot, and I have to say, you were a lucky man indeed."

That was enough to push the pain of crushed stones into the recesses of his mind. Marigold swung his legs around and was on his feet in a flash. His hand disappeared into the depths of Cezare's hood, gripping a neck he couldn't see. "Wife or not, I wouldn't wish your rotten cock on anybody."

A hearty laugh burst out from the cowl. Where the fuck was his face?

"What? What are you laughing at, wretch?"

"'Rotten cock'?" the voice snorted, unaffected by the strangling.

Marigold gripped harder still.

"So very childish."

"You've not seen me at my finest, sorcerer."

"Well, I suppose we shall meet face to face, soon."

"You're damn right we will."

And with that, Cezare's form disappeared. Marigold's fist clenched nothing in front of him but thin air. Fucking wizards. The woman that might well be Elvi was stood directly ahead, in the space that the form of Cezare had occupied.

Her grin was not a grin of this plane.

Her fist smashed Marigold in the nose. A fine mist of his blood coated her face. Marigold was reeling. That was four good hits she'd had on him now, and the nose was probably broken. Wasn't the first time for that, but it was going to be the last time she hit him. He staggered forwards, hand over his eyes, feigning delirium just for a moment.

Closer.

He looked below his palm, saw her feet near his.

Closer.

His arms shot out like striking snakes. He had her in his grasp. Hands wrapped tightly about her waist, but he didn't want to look her in the eye. This had to be done, and it could be done without watching. Marigold squeezed. He clenched his massive arms tighter and tighter. The bones in Elvi's spine began to shift. Creaks and groans the herald of the inevitable snap that was soon to come.

And then she laughed.

"You're all fucking mad! All of you!" Marigold bellowed, tightening his grip. "You're not my wife, woman. You need to go."

"Very well, my love."

The body writhed and wriggled. Her figure shifted and distorted from within Marigold's iron grasp. Her forehead smashed down onto Marigold's and she flew upwards, out of the vice. Marigold's hands went to his head. His skull was still one piece, thank fuck. Five blows, damn it. Where was she? Marigold swung left. He swung right. The room was empty. Bewildered, Marigold looked up. Elvi was clutching the ceiling, her mouth split in a devilish grin. Teeth that had been human moments ago were now sharp and vicious, and far too crowded in that delicate mouth.

"You are not my fucking wife!" Marigold reaffirmed.

Elvi dropped, fangs bared, fingers clawing air. Marigold opened his arms wide and let her come.

Her teeth sunk deep into Marigold's shoulder, but what was another bite mark after today? Her fingernails clawed shreds out of his back, but what were more scars after today? Her knees crashed into his ribs, but what were more broken bones after today? Let her have her fun. It was about to come to an end.

Slowly, almost imperceptibly, Marigold shuffled across the circular room, towards the bed. The biting and tearing continued, but Marigold weathered it. Wounds were to be avoided in battle, but when you took them, you took them like a fucking man. Wounds of the flesh and wounds of the mind, they all healed. Sometimes wounds were required in order to go on living, and Marigold wasn't planning on dying today. Not to this tower, this wizard, or the fucking demon gnawing on him. The bed was just beyond the thrashing limbs of the beast. It laughed maniacally, revelling in the violence. Perhaps Marigold and this new Elvi still had something in common.

Down he thrust her, onto the cruel twists of metal that formed the bedstead.

The laughing silenced. Her eyes widened. Her lips parted. Red bloomed from beneath her smock, followed by black shards of metal as the frame tore through her. Marigold found himself recoiling from the body, from the teeth that unhooked his flesh, from the fingers that ceased to dig in.

"Marigold," she wept, "I am your wife!"

"I just don't know how many times I have to say it," he said, looking at his feet rather than her.

"We are husband and wife!" she screamed as a fountain of blood erupted from her mouth.

Marigold gripped the creature once more, thrust her down further. "*You*," he growled viciously.

"Husband," she yelled simultaneously, amidst the tearing and scraping of flesh and bones.

"*Are*."
"And."
"*Not*."
"Fucking."
"*My*."
"Wife."
"*Wife*."

The creature's squirming stopped. The body went limp. The white sheets were stained beyond cleaning.

"Thank Greldin that's fucking done with," Marigold sighed. He was a shredded, tattered, and painful mess. But he was alive, and she was not. There was going to be some serious healing to come after he finished his work in this tower.

The body convulsed.

An awful laughter shook the ruined frame of the woman stuck to the end of the bed. Deep, inhuman, unhurt.

"Well, it was fun while it lasted," the voice spoke, twisting Elvi's throat as it spoke in tones not intended for her delicate vocal chords.

A black mist spewed forth, swirling overhead. It drifted across the room in all directions at once, and faded. Gone, whatever it was. A pained voice, Elvi's voice again, sobbed momentarily, and the body sagged for the last time. Her hands slumped onto the mattress as the last of her blood leaked away from her. Was there really something of her in there? Had she suffered death all over again?

Marigold forced himself to stare at the corpse. It was Elvi. And it wasn't. Was his wife, and it wasn't. Was human, and it wasn't. Marigold looked back to the ceiling again. Nothing there this time, thank fuck. His eyes moistened and the grey overhead blurred. He blinked hard and long, before any tears could form. He sniffed in firmly and breathed slowly out, quavering somewhat. Calm. One attempt at this was enough for any man, and he'd had two in one fucking day.

He dragged his weapons up from the edge of the room and approached the staircase. He climbed slowly. He climbed in silence.

THE BURIAL

The good thing about Marigold's camp was that its location on the hills of Illis granted a fine view of the land for miles around. The bad thing about it was that even while Marigold was still such a distance from it, he could see clearly that the settlement was burning and ruined. An orange sun rose through the woodland beyond the yurts, illuminating the devastation. Or was that just fire spreading? He dug his heels into the feathered rump of Sieg's rukh, rode her harder than she had ever been ridden before. There was so much he didn't want to see, and not a fucking thing he could do about it.

Eventually the rukh's talons began to slow their pounding of the earth. Smouldering yurts surrounded Marigold. The grass was ripped up, the trees and bushes were scorched, and the animal skins that made the tents were torn and rippling in the wind. Where was everyone? There had been a fight, that much was obvious, but unless that battle had been taken somewhere out of sight it seemed that it was over now, and had not gone in the clan's favour. Marigold expected there to be bodies. Where were they?

Where the fuck was everyone?

The morning was warm and bright, uncaring of the camp's plight. Marigold slid down from the back of his exhausted mount and let her wander off. Apparently, she felt that attending to some grass was more urgent than the scene of ruin that surrounded them. Of the three yurts before him, the closest one was the most intact. The smoke billowing from them was thicker than those further afield, suggesting they may have been among the last to have been attacked. Suggested potential for a recent clue as to what had happened. As Marigold paced slowly to the charred and flapping entrance of the tent, he noticed tiny footprints in the mud. Footprints like that of a baby, but a baby that was clearly very sure on its feet. On closer inspection, the blackened tent flap had a bloodied handprint smeared over the bottom corner. Adult sized. Victim sized.

Marigold pulled it open and stepped into the darkness.

He was surrounded by flies. The buzzing was incessant. They flew into his eyes, his ears, his mouth. What Pit-bred nonsense was this? Marigold slid forwards. Something slippery underfoot. Blood. The floor was slick with blood. The flies that weren't flying above it were stuck in it, buzzing desperately as they tried in vain to escape the tar pit that had claimed them. A fresh wind followed Marigold inside and swirled around, whipping up the smell of death, carrying it into Marigold's nasal cavity. As his eyes became accustomed to the humid gloom, he became aware of a white strip within the redness surrounding his feet. A bone. A rib. More white slashes bloomed from within the gore. More bones than one body could hold. A family. A severed hand still gripping a small dagger was enough to force Marigold out of the spoiled home.

He fell to his knees outside the yurt and drank deeply of the air.

That was not a way that anybody needed to meet their end. It didn't matter whether Greldin had set aside seats at his table for them or not. Marigold tried to convince himself that whatever life had lived within those unnameable bodies, it had to have been extinguished long before they had ended up in that state. It had to have been. He couldn't even fucking tell which of his clan it was that was in pieces in there. He'd seen a lot of death in his time, most of it could be attributed to himself, but this was different. These were his people.

He stumbled past more of the tents, almost tore the fucking skins from their frame as he gripped them to steady himself. There were pieces everywhere, but not enough to account for the entire populace of the clan. Some were obviously human, others were not, but what they were was hard to determine without the rest of them. Small, red, sharp. Eventually, one of the tents gave way to the staggering barbarian. It collapsed outwards and the skin that had been stretched over it tore free and wrapped itself around Marigold. He felt woozy. The morning was quickly becoming hot, but he was chilled to the bone. He stood bent over, hands on knees, drooling on the heat-browned grasses underfoot as the unwanted skin blanket clung to him. There were no voices on the wind, no screams, no cries for help. There were no survivors. What manner of fucking sorcery had been brought to his home? And why? Why the fuck had the sorcerer chosen Marigold's settlement? No provocation, not even any interactions with the prick. What had his clan done to deserve this? What *was* Cezare? Maybe that weasel-faced shit, Dahl, was lurking around somewhere, making sure his hellish plans were working out. Or was Dahl even Dahl? The bastard had arrived at the settlement alone, and there was no way that a pompous little prick like that would be able to travel a league in this land without being robbed or murdered by something. Was it Cezare all along? Marigold's head reeled with unanswered questions. He pulled himself up straight. The cunt's tower stood off in the distance, pale in the fading mist of the morning, but so much more of an obvious eyesore now than it had ever been before.

Marigold had to get to his tent.

He traipsed through mud churned to slush with blood and footprints. Prints from feet of varying sizes. Suffering for all ages. He wandered past fallen tents with the shapes of their owners reaching up from beneath the thin skins. He tottered between felled trees, splintered and smoking. Blood was everywhere. There hadn't been a fight at all, just a massacre. It didn't make sense. His people were strong, even the children could fight. Marigold's clan were a population that could hold their own. It was why they had been so successful, why they had grown, why nobody had ever thought to fucking bother them.

No. Marigold could see it now, so clearly.

He had become too confident. This was all his fault. He had spent too long in safety. Too many years of calm had dulled him, and his people had followed suit. His arrogance had spread a sense of invincibility among the clan. The years of strife that had brought the clan to where they were had become distant. Unnecessary.

And now it seemed that only he was left.

Marigold's yurt was ahead. A modest abode, no bigger than any of the others around it, but adorned with tattered wreathes of marigolds the colour of his hair at the threshold. A stupid fucking joke, like he was some delicate flower. Well, he *was* feeling pretty bloody delicate now. The tent pole in the centre of the structure was snapped and bent to one side, the top sagging inwards. An axe was wedged in the dirt before the closed entrance. Marigold kicked it aside and thrust Sear down in its place. If there was anything left of the enemy inside, Marigold was going to tear it apart with his teeth.

He pushed the limp cut of leather aside and ducked beneath.

Marigold vomited immediately. The little he had in his stomach pattered onto the torn-up rug underfoot.

Four naked and headless figures knelt in the centre of the room. They were arranged in a circle, holding hands. One, an adult woman. Two of them, girls on the verge of womanhood. The last was notably smaller than the rest, and facing the adult. Marigold staggered closer, lips quivering as shivers took each of his limbs. The four missing heads were piled in the middle of the circle, braided together with a tangle of black, red, and yellow hair. Marigold's lip quivered as he looked over each of the horrified faces in turn. He recognised all of the faces, but one of them stuck out somewhat more than the others.

Elvi.

Marigold's knees gave way, hitting the spine of the smallest and closest body. She fell stiffly to one side, dragging the rest of the circle down with her.

It wasn't easy digging a grave for anyone. It was especially difficult digging a grave for his wife, but Marigold cut the earth with all the rage and vigour he intended to apply to his upcoming attacks on Cezare's body. He didn't skimp on the depth. One by one, he brought out each of the bodies and lay them gently to rest alongside one another in the bottom of the pit. He couldn't just bury his wife, they were all his people. Elvi would be happy to share. The harsh light of day revealed more wounds on the bodies than had been visible in the murk of the tent. Decapitation hadn't been enough, it seemed, as each body was criss-crossed with slices from head to toe. Marigold choked as he found his thick fingers unable to untangle the thick clump of hair that held the heads together. He placed them atop the bodies.

The dirt was carefully piled on top until the corpses were covered. Between each scoop of soil, Marigold found himself glaring at Cezare's tower. He gritted his teeth and finished his work, laying one of the marigold wreathes from his yurt on top of the chopped earth.

There was no getting his wife back. No seeing her again in this life. No hearing her voice or holding her again from now until Marigold's death. All he could do was avenge her, and his ruined clan. If Greldin was the god Marigold knew Him to be, Elvi would be seated in His halls where she would await Marigold. Small fucking comfort that was right now, but slaying Cezare would almost certainly guarantee Marigold his place in the halls. If he hadn't earned it already.

Marigold remained in the stained jerkin he had travelled to and from Hvitstein in. He strapped a dagger to his boot and collected all of the vials of fuel for Sear that he had he could find in his yurt. Four of them. It was a big tower, but as long as he kept one back for Cezare he should be fine. He slid Sear into the wide sheath on his back and leapt onto Sieg's rukh. The bird was tired, but she was going to have to work a little harder today. Marigold swept his eyes across the wreck of his settlement. There wasn't much else to take, but he had his weapons and he had his rage, and that was all he really needed.

The tower didn't take long to reach, and Sieg's rukh was just as fired up as her rider by the time they arrived. Somehow, she seemed to understand what had happened. The huge structure was tall and slender and grey. No magical markings adorned it. No crude designs to ward off would-be-heroes. A shit wizard made his tower look dangerous, a good one didn't care. Or maybe Cezare was a shit one and knew how the good ones worked. All would be revealed soon.

As Marigold and his mount cleared the bushes that grew in a ring around the tower, he counted ten men loitering about the trimmed lawn. Not one of them seemed to be particularly alert. As Marigold and Sieg's rukh thundered into the clearing, they all scrambled to their feet, hastily brandishing swords and shields. Panicked heads darted this way and that, expecting more barbarians to rush from the undergrowth. Death was a twosome today. Marigold dropped down and charged in, holding Sear aloft as he screamed a guttural cry. Sieg's rukh trotted alongside him, squawking and screeching at the top of her lungs. Marigold swung Sear, cutting through the belly of the closest man. His innards spilled out quicker than he could collect them in his arms, his astonished eyes widened in horror as he watched the life rushing out of him and onto the grass. Marigold left the fucker to die like that. Sieg's rukh went straight for the face of the next one, tearing out a fatal chunk of nose and eyes and cheeks. She kicked a thick, yellow leg back as another of the men tried to get behind her, snapping his spine with a whiplash crack and sending him flying into a bush. Marigold lopped the arms from one, and the legs out from under another. The peaceful lawn was quickly descending into chaos. He sheathed Sear. One of the hapless shits began running for the tower door, shrieking for Cezare to save him. Marigold stormed after him.

"Bird," he barked, "deal with the rest of them."

The pathetic soldier beat upon the wooden doors. He turned around and threw his palms up just in time for Marigold's fist to split his face with a snap that sounded roughly like a neck going. The man went down and Marigold caught him under the arms. Where in the world had Cezare found these worthless fools? Marigold hoisted the body onto his shoulders and kicked the huge doors. They slowly creaked open, revealing little but a dull foyer on the other side. "Fucking thing wasn't even locked, you daft arsehole," he said to the lifeless body. Better to dump it inside, out of the rukh's view. He need that bird to deal with others. He didn't want her or any of those bastards following him inside whilst he went about his work.

Chapter Nine

TO ANOTHER DIMENSION

"Ah, so *you* killed *her*. That makes two of us."

Marigold lumbered up the final steps and into Cezare's study. "Of course I fucking killed it, damn you. There's no room in this world for anything that's had your rotten fingers on it. Or in it."

"Of course, Marigold," agreed Cezare, "though I suppose you'll have some trouble demolishing this tower all by yourself."

Marigold was too busy taking in the room to rise to that. This was a space that was much more along the lines of what he had expected from the tower in the first place. A classic wizard hole. The ceiling up here was higher than any of the lower floors, and a mezzanine jutted over half of the room. The walls, floor to mezzanine, were lined with shelves upon shelves of colourful spines of more books than Marigold believed he could count. Not that he needed to count them, for he knew each and every page would be filled with magical fucking nonsense. It all needed burning, all of it. He noted the flickering candles that dripped on stands dotted around the room as a possible catalyst for that. Beyond the shelves, narrow windows admitted strips of moonlight into the centre of the room, made solid with particles of ancient book pages. At the far end of this final chamber, between the beams of pale night light, waited the condemned man himself. He stood behind a dark, wooden lectern. A huge book was spread open on the thing. One of Cezare's bony fingers was held mid-page. Evidently, Marigold had interrupted him in his work.

"We're going to end this right now, you stoneless sack of shit," spat Marigold.

"Well, Marigold, *you* can end it."

Marigold lowered his brow, trying to look every way at once. What did the cunt have in store for him now? Spears from the floor? Wives from the shelves? Pit spawn from the pages? Cezare pulled back the black cowl from around his face. Finally, the object of Marigold's rage was fully revealed. The prick was young. To look at, at least. His black hair hung in greasy clumps to either side of his youthful, white face. A pitiful attempt at a beard grew in fits and starts across his cheeks and chin. A red pimple here and there suggested he might really have been in his teen years. How long had this baby been off his mother's teat? Well, it didn't bloody matter what age he was. A cunt was a cunt, and this dumb cunt needed killing. Cezare's brutal death was what Marigold had been craving since that witch Adia had dropped his name.

Marigold stepped toward Cezare. Immediately, his feet were replaced with a cascade of agony.

"You could stand to be a little more observant, my friend," sneered Cezare. "Well," he laughed, "you'll be *standing* right there for some time." The wizard gleefully pointed to Marigold's feet.

Marigold stared in bewilderment at the blood flowing over the top of his boots. Amidst the dark liquid, silver shards arranged in a cross shape covered each foot. Hooks. He was fucking hooked to the floor. At least it made the pain in his back seem somewhat inconsequential now. Blood from the wounds streamed into narrow grooves cut into the stones beneath them, coursing its way across the room. It surrounded an angular white sketch in the space between the barbarian and the Pit-meddler. Marigold said nothing. He locked eyes with Cezare. The sorcerer began to flow across the room, his dark robes showing barely a hint of the legs moving inside. Maybe the fucker didn't even have legs, maybe stoneless wasn't even too far from the truth.

"Marigold, Marigold, Marigold," chanted Cezare as he came to a stop at arm's length from him. "You know, I spent such a long time searching for a man like you, and here you finally are. Stood before me, handing over all of that delightful blood I need. I've been keeping an eye on you for some time, you know? I was so pleased when I acquired this small amount of your blood on the contract from Dahl that you... signed. But I needed more."

"Thought as fucking much."

"Heroes are few and far between these days. Well, the ones that like to make their actions well-known. You know? The vain ones? The ones that only ever do anything so that others think more highly of them? Slaying a white gargunnoch, for instance. That's big stuff. That's you, Marigold."

"Aye, I suppose it is." There was no point denying it, it was why he was here and his wife and clan were all dead. "If only it had been a fucking gargunnoch."

"Ha, yes. That's why Dahl is just an apprentice. You know, Marigold, I honestly didn't expect you to actually make it all the way up my tower to find me, but there we go."

"Didn't do your bloody research properly then, did you?" Marigold spat. "I've murdered more than one or two of your fucking kind before."

"Sometimes, Marigold, you just have a make a guess at the protection you'll need, and sometimes those estimates are found wanting. It's all part of the learning process. What a waste of good skags and roughskins this has been, though. Fortunately, I already have another

Bloodmaster waiting in the wings and… Oh, did you happen to run into Dahl? I had plans for that fellow."

With the speed of a striking snake, Marigold tore Sear from his back and swung the deadly blade across Cezare's neck. The wizard collapsed into grey dust, reforming several paces further back. Marigold blinked. Little shit seemed to be prepared for everything. Probably better not to throw her at him, then.

"Now, now. You're at the disadvantage, remember? Not I," Cezare chided, waggling a finger in mock admonishment. "All you need to do is let your blood flow for me. That's really all I've needed since I found you! Those goats were all well and good, but your blood is the main event. You know, you could have made this so much easier for yourself if you'd just let my creatures take care of you, but, here you are, hooked and stuck like a fish out of water. What a waste of good coin Korag was, and so eager too. But Marigold, I suppose I should thank you. You've let me know just how incapable those imbeciles were before I had to pay them again."

"You talk too fucking much, you know that?"

"I enjoy words, Marigold, and there so few to share them with. Those barbaric roughskins speak only in grunts and lisps, and only wanted to speak of you. I know enough about you already, but there's a little more to me than just wanting you. You're a means to an end. An end I have been working on for some time. There are planes upon planes of knowledge out there, you know? Realms of power and wisdom. Why content myself to the paltry excuse we have for an existence here in Rosaria, when the lives of a handful of men will allow me to traverse the other ways and learn from them?"

Marigold shook his head and sheathed Sear with a sigh. "Why are there never any decent men or women with wands and spell books and… and fucking chalk circles on the floor?" he asked, mainly speaking to himself. "What is it about you pricks that always sees you turn to evil? I won't complain about having a body to butcher, but just once it would be good to meet a fucking spellcaster content with conjuring up a plate of meat and a horn of ale."

"Evil, Marigold?" asked Cezare. The bastard looked genuinely perplexed. "I suppose you would see it that way. A man such as myself has the ability to gain power beyond the ken of normal men such as yourself."

Marigold breathed slowly and let the arsehole continue. Couldn't the fucker have just slashed his throat and been done with it? Would have been quicker for the wizard. Would have saved Marigold's last remaining ear from this barrage of rukh shit.

"With more abilities at my disposal, fewer things are out of reach for me. Naturally, I then try to bring those few things that are out of reach, into reach. It is an academic pursuit, Marigold. And – I know, I can see it in your confused, barbarian face – the methods available to me appear to be brutal, but if you had had the joy of conversing with beings higher than yourself, to be spoken to as an equal of the same, superior level of existence, then you, too, would come to understand that a few hundred deaths are nothing." Cezare snapped his fingers in delight. "A blink of an eye, a passing thought. That's all you and your clan are. The Gods that I speak with acknowledge my work as training, they understand that I have done what I can with the materials available to me in this realm, and they want to see me do more, with more. I have an important future ahead of me, Marigold, and it shall come to be known to everyone."

"You really do love a fucking monologue, eh?"

"Very droll, Marigold."

"Aye, I've a knack for that, and shame for you that I knew exactly what you were about before you vomited it all over me."

The grooves within the white circle on the floor were almost full with Marigold's blood. All things considered, he had lost a lot of blood today. Must be the fury that was keeping him from keeling over. Or those fucking hooks. The room began to rumble gently, like the very foundations of the tower were being shaken by some gigantic creature outside.

"Now what the fuck is happening, Cezare?" Marigold asked wearily. "What have you done?"

"Aha," laughed Cezare, "thought you knew what I was about? Your blood is special, you know?"

"How? Blood's blood. You have one man's, you have it all."

"Not so, my large friend. I need the blood of the hateful."

"Hateful? I think you're giving yourself too much credit. I want you dead – and I'll have you dead – but I'll soon forget about you once it's done."

"Oh, I don't need *you* to hate *me*, you nincompoop," Cezare chuckled.

Marigold sighed again. So that was it. He couldn't deny it. He wasn't too fond of himself at all at the moment. Lured in by glory and prizes, left his wife to be murdered, condemned his clan to ruin and death. He shifted his feet within the spikes. His great thighs clenched, failing to move him anywhere beyond the spot to which he was rooted. He could tear them off, but would be he able to reach Cezare after that? He was just going to have to watch, for now. "And just what is it that you're going to do? Enslave the world? Kill everyone? That's the usual idiocy planned by your fucking type."

"All in good time, Marigold," the wizard shouted above the growing din. "Today, I'm merely going to visit my masters, and my masters do not inhabit this realm." Cezare stood in the middle of the circle. He raised his arms, and the rumbling grew. Chunks of stone and grit began to fall from above. Books fell from the shelves, splaying out on the ground below.

"So that's the demonic shit you were playing at with my clansmen? Just trying it out, were you?"

"Oh, I never got to see the results! How were they?"

"Pathetic. Everything that came out is dead."

"Oh, well, I suppose only the smallest of them would have been able to travel through such bodies," Cezare said quietly, thoughtfully. "You may have seen some at your camp? The goats were much too small to keep the portals open though... But, good to hear that the concept behind the summoning worked!"

The shaking seemed to reach a crescendo.

A red line split the air. It began to twist, spreading a red oval across the centre of the room, right over the circle design below. The pages of the book on the lectern began to flip rapidly, though no wind rushed. The portal stopped twisting. It stood twice the height of Marigold, shimmering as it revealed a barren, red-brown land beyond. The black skies inside churned and growled, as though they were as much alive as anything else that awaited in there. Marigold felt his confidence ebbing away along with the blood from his feet. The Pits. A fucking hole straight to the Pits, and a large one this time. It wasn't often that he thought he might not win.

"I'll be back soon, Marigold," Cezare said. "You could try praying while I'm gone. It won't help, but you may feel that it is of some comfort. I may be a little… different, when I return."

"Pray? Fucking pray? Who in the Pits do you think I am, you wretched prick? Greldin is my God, and a barbarian that calls for aid isn't a fucking barbarian at all."

"Suit yourself."

"Think about what you're about to fucking do, you dumb cunt!" Marigold yelled. "Only a moon-crazed fuckwit with a truly deluded sense of importance messes with shit like this! What do you think's gonna happen? A demon's going to shake hands with you and hand all his power over? It's going to fucking devour you, and then whatever comes back is going to be *it*, not *you*! What a fucking waste of your life. What a fucking waste of Elvi's life! Of my fucking clan! You're a dead cunt, Cezare, either way now, you're fucking dead!"

Cezare looked back at Marigold once and shrugged. He stepped into the portal and was gone.

"Fuck. Fuck! *Fuck*!" Marigold crouched down, examining his feet. The metals were like tiny grappling hooks, and they appeared to have moving parts. The initial spike went up, and then the sides shot out. Moving parts were weaker than one solid piece. Moving parts could be broken. He slid his dagger from his boot and began wedging it into the tiny hinges of the contraption. He alternated quick glances between his feet and the swirling mass of hell in the middle of the room. The pain had reached the point of numbness, and he wasn't particularly concerned about it increasing while Cezare was getting away. He hadn't climbed all this way just to let the bastard go free. He hadn't impaled the body of his wife on a bed just so Cezare could do the same to someone else someday. A shard of metal pinged off across the room. Three pieces remained of the hooks over his right foot. He worked hard, he worked fast. A clatter signalled the next piece coming away, then the next. He bent the final piece off with his bare hands and slid his foot out over the top of it. "That's gonna take some fucking healing when I'm out of here," he grumbled. The second foot was released faster still, and Marigold found himself stood before the twisting portal.

His heart pounded within his beaten chest. Even a man as brave as he hesitated for a moment before stepping in. There were many unknowns. He could see the other side from here, but could he come back from it? Could he breathe in there? Well, if that coward had dared to rush in, Marigold would probably be alright too.

Probably.

Marigold jumped through.

The heat hit him immediately. Close, humid, crushing air. Sulphurous to the taste and so hot in his lungs that it didn't feel like air at all. But he was breathing, not choking. It would do. Salty sweat drenched him, running into each and every wound, washing him with a fresh wave of agony. The furious black clouds were low, bubbling overhead like molten metal. Vast, leathery stems reached up into them, though what they were Marigold knew not. The sand was red and hot, clinging to Marigold's bloodied feet. Iron-grey rocks jutted out of it like natural daggers, reaching across the land as far as he could see. Dust devils twirled here and there. Between the nearest trunk-like structure and Marigold lay a flabby heap of flesh and blood. A heap that had tentacles stretching off into the dust around it, gripping in as though for purchase. A number of those red imp bastards danced atop the mass, shrieking and tearing. Marigold had often wondered what the Pits he cursed so often were like, and now he wished that he didn't know them at all. Whatever Cezare thought lived here, Marigold strongly doubted anything more than savagery from any of them.

And coming back to that fucker, Cezare had been out of sight for far too long. But the pissant had left footprints that hadn't yet been blown away. They led off, into the forest of jagged rocks, halfway to the horizon. Marigold gave chase as fast as he could on his ruined feet, glancing back at the portal frequently, reassuring himself that it was still there. Roars and hisses filled the air, coming from what might well be an entire menagerie of unseen creatures. More meat for his blade if the shits came his way. One of the titanic, leathery stems began to lift up into the roiling clouds, bending in the middle. A fucking knee! It was so huge as to appear that it was moving in slow motion. Marigold stared up in amazement as the belly of the beast above broke through the cloud barrier. It made a gargunnoch seem like a mouse. The floor shook so violently as the enormous foot came down that Marigold was cast to the ground, earning a mouthful of bitter, red sand as he rolled amidst the quaking.

"Can't be fucking doing with that again and again!" he shouted, his voice tiny among the native sounds. As if it would stop for an insignificant thing like him, whatever it was. He was less than an ant to it.

But the immense leg and foot did not immediately move again.

Marigold resumed the chase. Most of the footprints had been shaken away by the great creature, but enough remained that Marigold was able to follow them between the rocks. Tall and rough, the stones rent the ground like great teeth. And who the fuck was here to say there weren't gums below the dust? A grunting from behind drew Marigold's attention. A squat beast, shoulder-height with Marigold, trotted into the space between the rocks, blocking the way back. Two great, grey horns protruded from its head, sharp and ready to stab. Beady, yellow eyes looked Marigold up and down with consideration. For Marigold's part, he decided that being tossed overhead and onto the forest of spines decorating the beast's back was not for him. He crouched a little, coiled, ready to react. The monster stomped its thick feet at the challenge, kicking the dirt underfoot up into a minor storm. It bellowed a throaty wail and pounded toward Marigold. The fucker must have weighed more than a couple of rukhs, for Marigold felt the earth – or whatever it was – tremble beneath his pained soles. He dragged Sear out and held her ready, metal point aimed at horn point. The beast ran dead on into the blade, open mouth first. It stopped with a groan and a rattle in its throat.

"Big, vicious, and fucking stupid." Marigold drew Sear from the unfortunate's maw and swung hard through the hot air to clear the black blood that dripped from her. "I thought as much." Without further ado, Marigold plucked one of the vials from his belt and dropped it into her hilt. The flames weren't going to make the place any hotter, but they might deter anything else that got in his way.

He followed the twisting sand between the stones and finally came upon a clearing. Within it was his mark. Cezare knelt, head down, chanting some unintelligible tongue. Standing before the sorcerer was a bipedal monster. Red-skinned and goat-legged. Slender, yet muscular, thick arms the length of Marigold himself. The head was akin to a fucking dog of all things. Long snout, intelligent eyes, sharp teeth. Just like a dog, save for the array of black horns decorating its brow. He wasn't going to look at the simple hound in the same way again.

"Cezare," he yelled, pushing the top of his hilt in and crushing the vial inside. "This is it!" He ran towards the pair, dragging his blade in the sharp sand to ignite the fluid. The demon hissed loudly at Marigold as Sear burst into glorious flame. The barbarian rounded on the pair. He thrust her deep into the stomach of the musclebound horror and drew upwards. Black blood gushed forth, stringy innards spilled over the ground, bathing Cezare in its demonic gore. Marigold yanked his sword out and swung up at the devil's neck. The dog-head fell to the sand with a thud, throwing up a small cloud that settled in a congealed mess. Dead. Some fucking demon that had been. He had known grandparents fight harder. Cezare, who had been laughing maniacally throughout the whole episode, turned to face Marigold and stood up.

"This is it!" Cezare cried, coated in black liquid. "It is done! I can feel it! I can feel everything!"

"Then you'll feel this," Marigold roared, and hurled his massive, hilt-grasping fist right between Cezare's eyes.

Marigold thought hard about his next move as the pimpled wizard slumped to the dust in an unconscious heap. Cezare was going to die, there was no changing that, but Marigold quickly decided that getting out of this hell hole sooner rather than later was preferable. It was all well and good relieving the bastard of his head right here and now, but he wanted to enjoy this kill, and he simply couldn't do that while his escape from this realm was in question. Like the guard on his shoulder upon entering the tower, Marigold hauled Cezare up. But the sorcerer wasn't going to escape with just a severed arm and leg, oh no, though he *would* remain intact until he woke up again. Marigold reckoned on him being quite surprised when he eventually came to. Sear still blazed, held firm in Marigold's fist. Few men could wield such a magnificent weapon with one hand, but Marigold was one of them. Even so, Cezare certainly felt as though he was getting heavier. And bigger. Fuck, he was just tired. Exhausted. It would all be over soon.

The portal still churned, far away in the open red desert. It shimmered as it appeared to turn in place. What if it was on the verge of winking out? Marigold made his final dash, paying little heed to the spears of pain in his feet and legs. A mob of marauding imps scattered in all directions with screeches of terror as Marigold thundered on through the middle of the pack, clutching his prize. Little shits seemed less daring on their home turf. Dirt. Sand. Whatever. Beyond the portal, off in the distance, one of the colossal legs began to rise, again in slow motion. It wasn't the only one either, now that Marigold studied the horizon. He sprinted for all his worth, not taking any chances on having his prey knocked from his shoulder in this strange land. Cezare was not getting a chance to wake up here, not where Marigold was at a disadvantage. The portal loomed as Marigold staggered through the last few steps towards it, somehow bigger here than it was back in Illis. With a bellow and a last surge of his strength, Marigold hurled the limp and unconscious wizard through the gateway.

Chapter Ten

VISCERA

Cezare's limp body slapped the tower floor as Marigold leapt through the portal after him. The sorcerer's arms were flung out in the rough landing, scraping a gap through the white mural below the portal. In a soundless instant, the path to another dimension scrunched up and vanished. Marigold shot a glance at the once shimmering space, mouthed a curse and whistled with relief. Even he wouldn't have been so rough with Cezare had he known that he had risked cutting himself off.

Marigold swung his flaming sword in his hand, limbering up for the finale. The barbarian was tense. This was it. Time to cut the shithead up. Too bad the magical bastard was still out cold, but Marigold was starting to tire of the whole fiasco anyway. Down came his blade, point aimed at an arm.

The body slid out from under Marigold as Sear bit the stones instead.

"The fuck?" he spat with indignation.

Cezare still appeared to be unconscious, despite his sudden jerk. Whatever. Marigold could cut him up here, he could cut him up there, it was all the same to him. He readied Sear to strike once again.

Cezare slid across the dusty stone with a whoosh, back to where he had come from.

"What's this, then? You got some chant that keeps you safe while you're asleep?"

"We haven't taught him that yet," came a reply from the body, a reply far too deep for the young cocksucker's delicate vocal chords.

"And who are you, then?" Marigold asked. "That dog-headed cunt I tore apart between the rocks? Fucking knew that had been too easy."

Cezare's body began to twist and stretch. Limbs distorted with sickening cracks. The wizard's legs – and it appeared that he did have legs – protruded out from under his robes, bending backwards at the knee like the hindquarters of a goat. Five toes congealed into two, black-taloned digits. The sorcerer's arms reached up into the air, weirdly long and nauseating to look at in their pallid glory. The body began to stand up, the space where its stones should have been – and there were none, the barbarian noted – stood level with Marigold's head, hips twice as wide as the warrior. With a revolting snap the chest and arms and head followed suit, rearing up and filling the floor, almost tall enough to touch the mezzanine ceiling above. Cezare's head seemed to fall in on itself, and as his features sunk inside his skull, a pale white snout began to emerge. Black eyes replaced human ones. Ears began to droop, long and thin. Black spikes protruded in some demonic pattern across the forehead. The transformation looked fucking agonising, like the kind where the one afflicted would welcome death long before the process was complete.

The creature breathed and sighed. It snarled and sniffed at the air, its mutated larynx ushered rumbles not meant for a human body. The demon stood more than twice as high as Marigold. It flexed its rapidly swelling muscles. Dark veins coursing with foreign blood pulsed up and down each limb. The monster heaved as it began to laugh a deep, evil laugh. This was the demon from beyond, alright.

"Well, look at the fucking size of you," Marigold swallowed. "How in the world are you planning on leaving through that door? He motioned Sear to the exit behind him, and gave a second thought to making a dash for it himself. He'd been in countless fights, but the one that was about to begin gave him real cause for concern. But he wouldn't run. If he was to die here, so be it, but that thing from beyond wasn't going to kill him without earning a few scars of its own.

The laughing ended abruptly, and the head snapped to glare at Marigold. "You won't be needing that," it said in a voice almost too deep to understand. It swept its snake-like arm across the room. The flames of Sear were immediately doused.

In almost-panic, Marigold shoved his penultimate vial into Sear's hilt, and chipped her tip against the stones at his feet. Flames burst forth, stronger than before.

"Didn't we just say you won't be needing that, human?" The demon barked harshly and cast its arm to the side again, whipping up a wind that knocked Marigold from his feet and sent Sear spinning from his hand and across the room. She wedged herself in the shelves, immediately igniting the books within. The crackling fire began to eat through the pages and spines and covers. At least something good had come from that. "Your flames are nothing to us, mortal. We were conceived in fires hotter than you could imagine!"

"So, your Pa had cockrot then?" Marigold quipped through clenched teeth as he pulled himself back up. "Doesn't look like it could have been passed on, though."

"Ah, a jester. Cezare thought as much too."

That seemed a tad unfair. "And Cezare is happy with this arrangement, dog?"

"The mage is merely a passenger. We have assumed control of this vessel and bent it to our means.

With Cezare's magic, we are unlimited. We will soon be fully reborn into your world, and you will long for death. You all will, even before our master joins us."

Marigold felt like a naughty child before an angry adult. An adult that had yet more, bigger adults stood behind it. The end was about to begin, no matter which way he looked at it. "Well," he shouted, trying his best to keep his voice steady, "you'd better save me a fucking piece of the cunt, because when I'm done with you, I'm ending him!"

Its thundering laughter began to fill the room.

What the fuck was he supposed to do now? Sear was still swaying in the wall; the fire was spreading over the door. All he had was a pissing dagger. Well, nothing for it. He wasn't dying like some dog when it was a dog that loomed before him. Marigold tore out the blade and ran. He leapt toward it. Fingernails plunged into the monster's knee as he launched himself up onto its chest. He wrapped his arms around the girthy trunk as best he could and set about his work of stabbing.

The pit-spawn took its punishment in silence as Marigold slid his dagger in and out. Wounds gaped open but little blood flowed; the demon seemed only vaguely aware of the gashes that would have slain Marigold ten times over, until finally his tiny weapon struck something hard. The demon howled a screech that shook the room. Burning books fell from the shelves and fire began to creep across the floor. A great hand, fingers longer than Marigold's arm, gripped the barbarian's back and plucked him from the chest. Marigold found himself airborne, unable to tell which way was up. His head cracked stone. Stars burst into his vision, but through it he could make out the ceiling overhead. It looked different. Lower. He was up on the mezzanine. The highest point of the bloody tower. Some arm that bastard had on it to lug him up here. To his side stood Cezare's bed. A huge, soft thing that took up most of the space here. Fucking typical that he'd missed that. He still held his dagger, somehow. Would have been nasty if he'd landed on that. Marigold pulled himself up, rubbing the back of his head, watching the blurred form of the demon Cezare striding up the curved stairs to find him. The leggy bastard took six in one step, but was forced to crouch as it reached the top. Marigold ducked by the side of the bed, waiting for the arsehole to stop and look. The head lurched from side to side, searching.

There it was.

Marigold dashed with the speed of a wildcat. He leapt up and thrust his dagger into the space where he assumed Cezare's stones might once have been. No sweet spot lay there anymore. Instead, Marigold found himself flying again.

The floor below hit him much harder than the wall had. That was at least one rib snapped, probably more. Marigold rolled onto his side, coughing and spluttering, shaking his head. If he managed to live to tell this story, he was going to have to tell it fucking differently. Blood seeped out from between his teeth. He spat it to the floor, just in time to see it appear to shrink away as he was hauled up from it, back into the air. Huge hands squeezed. Rings grew in his vision. The pressure he felt was immense, but Marigold's iron muscles held back the very worst.

"We'll eat," said the hellish voice.

That was all he fucking needed. Tenderised and shaped, and here was the end of it. Made shitty sense, and evidently the spawn of the Pits liked their meat rare.

Hot, stinking breath leaked from the demon's maw. Teeth like daggers glistened in the firelight.

Daggers. Dagger? His dagger!

Marigold kicked and Marigold flailed. The great arms twitched and he freed himself for a moment. Down he fell, but not for long. The hands snatched him again, but the dagger in the empty crotch was now in reach. He swung an arm and grabbed it. Up he was hauled. The jaws stretched open. Marigold clutched the dagger tightly, awaiting the right moment.

Now.

Into the demon's throat he thrust. Again, again, again. He twisted with lightning reflexes, tens of wounds in the space of seconds. Veins and sinew were dragged out with each stab, flopping and swinging below the wounds. The demon bellowed, but its voice was shaky. Blood or not, he'd torn something tasty. He fumbled with his belt, tucking the dagger, catching the top of his thigh as he snatched Sear's last vial; a miracle it wasn't already smashed. It was a long shot, but the options he had were become scarcer by the moment. Marigold wriggled and shook, managing to wedge an arm between two monstrous teeth. The jaws snapped shut. The top row pierced the arm, but it was too far between the teeth for anything worse than a flesh wound. He clenched his arm and pulled himself closer. He sunk the vial of incendiary liquid deep into the hole in demon Cezare's throat, crushing his palm into a fist. He felt shards of glass tear into his hand, felt the viscous liquid run between his fingers. He yanked his arm out, leaving the shards inside. The jaws above chomped, the head snapped back. This was his one and only chance. The arm between the teeth was getting quickly torn up, and in seconds it was going to be useless, if it even remained attached at all. His free fingers searched for his dagger. Success! He began stabbing again, as fast as a viper. Aiming for one of the shards, anything to make a spark.

Stab.

Marigold felt the fingers in the mouth snap.

Stab.

The inhuman hands around his waist crushed tighter.

Stab.

Something began to pull at his legs, trying to tear him apart.

Stab.

A spark. A flash. A flame shot out from within the wound.

Marigold screamed as his hand caught alight. He was mid-flight again. The burning liquid ran down his arm and a strip of flame ate into his jerkin. Marigold crashed back to the stone, just as his jerkin erupted in a blaze. As he tore wildly to free himself from a fiery death, the demon Cezare thrashed around, clutching at its burning throat. The beast's arms flailed this way and that as it smashed into the wall behind it. Huge chunks fell away, revealing the night sky outside. The mutated Cezare roared as he fell to the floor. Marigold, naked as the day he was born but for his boots, lumbered towards his downed foe. Seemed that he was destined to face the cunt with his stones bared after all; this rebirth he had considered was becoming more literal than he had intended. He danced around the remaining flames and stood by the snout. Slowly at first, he began to punch and kick at the body. The stench of burning, demonic flesh began to fill the upper reaches of the tower. Marigold continued raining down blows upon his enemy. Then, without any warning, a black and misty cloud spewed forth from Cezare's eyes and mouth and nose. It swirled together overhead, forming a hideous mass that churned the air. It groaned for a heartbeat, then dissipated in all directions. Marigold looked down at the body.

It began to shrink.

Slowly, and noisily, it began to reform into the choking form of the human Cezare. He slumped onto his front, blood gushing from the hole in his throat. Fingers delved into the dripping blood, desperately trying to draw glyphs on the floor. The cunt was trying to save himself.

"No," said Marigold plainly, and dragged his foot through the impromptu design.

Cezare tried again, and again Marigold stopped him. The sorcerer slumped onto his face, arms weakly shaking about him, fingers twitching, unable to function as the mind so frantically intended. Cezare's young lips began to move.

"What's that you're saying, Cezare? Was it fucking worth it? Didn't I bloody tell you it would end up this way?"

The lips continued to move, repeating the same motions again and again.

Marigold crouched, put his good ear to the quickly expiring wizard.

"Mother," Cezare whispered.

Marigold recoiled and stood back up. "They're your final words? Just how fucking old are you? I want you to beg. Beg for your life, you bastard!" he screamed. He coiled his broken fingers into a fist and punched. The blows were unending, each one left the face of Cezare a little less human-looking. "Beg! Demand forgiveness!" There was little left but pulp beneath Marigold's knuckles. He really was going to have to tell this story differently.

The lips stopped moving, as did the eyes. Cezare was dead.

The fire in the room was cowed by the winds that rushed in through the fissures in the outer wall. A couple more books fell from the shelves, burning nothing but themselves as their pages flicked back and forth in the draughts. The final movements in a room that had seen far too much ceased. Marigold fell back onto his naked arse. The stone was cold. It was actually soothing. He breathed lightly, trying to avoid the sharp pains in his ribs. He felt like he'd been beaten like a goat steak. As he gave his body a once over, he realised what a mess he was. It was a wonder he was still conscious, come to think about it. His left arm was in tatters; huge gashes ripped into the flesh, blood pouring profusely from the wounds. Several fingers required splints. His left eye was starting to dim, being pushed shut by the swollen flesh around it. Blood covered him from head to toe, but whether it was all his or some of Cezare's he couldn't tell. Slowly and slovenly, Marigold dragged himself up the stairs to the sheets of Cezare's bed. He tore at the white fabric as best he could and made himself several makeshift bandages. There wasn't enough for his modesty. What a fucking sight he must have been: leather boots, cock and stones swinging free, and blood pouring from every inch.

He staggered back down the steps and found himself at Cezare's lectern. Somehow, amidst all of the chaos that had just ransacked the room, Cezare's demonic book remained open and intact on the platform. Marigold took it up and held it in his hands. The binding was soft. A nose and ear adorned the back of the cover. The bloody thing was bound in the skin from some poor sap's head. He flicked idly through the pages. Marigold was learned enough to be able to read, but none of the letters inside made a lick of sense. As he stared at some of the diagrams his head began to pound. Fucking magic. The demon had mentioned a master. Perhaps knowledge of this master lurked somewhere within this foul tome? Marigold wasn't strong enough yet, but maybe one day that demonic fucker would be fair game. He closed the volume and took it under his arm. Someone would be able to read it. Somewhere. He swayed as he made his way to the smouldering shelves by the door. He pulled Sear free and elected to carry her under his other arm now that her sheath had gone up in flame. It was a pity that the fire had gone out. Perhaps he would be able to start something more destructive when he was back outside.

"Well, at least I'm still fucking standing," he said in a voice merely half as loud as he had intended. "I win, Cezare. You fucking hear me? Prick." He hoped the bastard had felt every blow whilst he was passenger for the demon. Marigold looked back around the devastated room. What a sight. Between the gaps in the stone of the ruined wall, the stars of Greldin's Axe hung in the cold, night sky. Maybe the bastard really had been watching over him all along. To be honest, there weren't many other ways in which Marigold could explain his continued survival.

Marigold hobbled down the stairs, his stones slapping noisily against his thighs.

Past the corpse of a duplicated wife he walked, through the empty floor where Dahl had attacked him. The sixth floor was bare save for the corpses of young roughskins. As he wound his way down to the fifth, Marigold tripped on something. Korag, dead on the steps. The dagger Marigold had thrown to him wedged in his throat. Sightless bastard had probably fallen down as he attempted to find his way out. What a shit way to go.

The warrior walked too slowly to slip on the bloodied floor where he had fought the imps and tentacles. The bodies were a mess, pieces strewn everywhere. Better to burn the damn tower than try and reassemble and bury each man, woman, and child. Marigold hopped over fat leeches and kicked at the corpse of the Bloodmaster on the fourth. One of the skags still smouldered down on floor three, seems they made decent fuel. He tiptoed carefully through the spears of the second. Dead or not, he didn't want Cezare to have the last laugh. Finally, he was back on the ground floor. The dead guard still lay there, white and stiff, surrounded by a pool of his own blood.

Marigold found himself at the doors held fast by the arm and a leg. "What next then?" he asked the limbs, positive that this really was the bottom floor this time. A couple of weeks ago he hadn't been particularly interested by the reports of wrongdoings out in the world, but he did recall talk of a Tall Man causing no end of trouble to the north. Well, he was a free agent now, and the Pits knew he needed something to occupy himself with. He watched his bare cock and stones swing in the draught that swept through the cracks between the doors. Free in more than one way. Not like he had anything to be ashamed of. He was going to have to earn some fucking coin though. Hadn't had to do that in years. Perhaps there were still some clothes back at the camp; a fine sight he'd make walking into a village like this. With Sear and book held tightly between his knees, he tore at the arm and the leg, snapping the arm into two pieces before it came loose. The doors fell open of their own accord, revealing Sieg's rukh. She was pecking at entrails that seeped from splits in a twisted corpse. A gold necklace lay coiled by it. Dahl. So it had been real.

"Good work, Sofia," Marigold said.

After

THE TALE RETOLD

Marigold sat listening, inside his great yurt,
Men came far and wide to tell of their hurts.
Goats had gone missing across the whole land,
The farmers sought Marigold, for he'd understand.

Nought Marigold could do without further ken,
He bade the farmers to tighten their pen.
Away each one went, grumbling and sad,
And into the tent came a weasel-faced lad.

Dahl was his name, slimy and thin,
Had news of a contract to interest them in.
A great white gargunnoch ripe for the killing,
Payments to be made, if Marigold was willing.

A hunt for a beast was Marigold's delight,
He agreed to destroy it and end poor Dahl's plight.
Away Marigold rode, with Vik, Sieg, and Haggar,
To lands far off they carried their swagger.

But the beast was not what it had been named,
Marigold swore that the fucker was tamed.
Not a fight it put up out there in the fields,
Quickly, so swiftly, the creature did yield.

Against his better judgement they cut off its head,
To take as a trophy despite being misled.
The town of Hvitstein welcomed with glee,
Relief at this kill so plain to see.

The head of the settlement demanded they stay,
And by the next morning they'd arrange them their pay.
Marigold looked to the left and the right,
Something was off, and it didn't seem right.

The dusk became darkness, the party began,
The women were wild, Sieg and Vik formed a plan.
Marigold sat quietly, no woman for him,
His wife was back home, his expression was grim.

Something was wrong, some devilry alright,
He stormed out the inn, and into the night.
Marigold checked on the rukhs in the barn,
And found an old man trying to do them great harm.

Marigold snapped the fellow's thin neck,
And the last living rukh dealt her own savage peck.
The warrior rushed to his men in the tavern,
Found each of them dead in the lust-filled cavern.

The woman that greeted him on his arrival,
Claimed that Marigold's men would form their revival.
The wizard Cezare had given them power,
Upon the young woman laid Marigold's glower.

But the youthful leader was in fact an old witch,
And Marigold sheared the head from the bitch.
He leapt on the rukh, fleeing the city alone,
And rode hard as he could, back to his home.

Disaster awaited, and he knew there'd be death,
But the sight that met him stole all of his breath.
Slain was his wife, gone were his clan,

Ruined were the yurts, he was the last man.

He buried his woman and took what he could,
Glared at horizon, where the wizard's tower stood.
He'd ruin the bastard, tear limb from limb,
And from the cunt's shoulders, his head he would trim.

Before the tower our warrior stood,
To rid the land of wizards for good.
Through the doors he stormed his way,
That fucking Cezare was going to pay.

The tower he locked with an arm and a leg,
From a guard he brought in, by the Pits did he beg.
Into the stairs did Marigold run,
Looking forward to having his fun.

Floor two was dark and gloomy and dim,
There was nothing to fight, there nothing to skin.
A hand burst forth, as that of a ghost,
And wrapped its talons around his throat.

Marigold staggered, tried not to breathe,
But try as he might he could not heave,
The Pit-chilled grasp from 'round his neck,
Marigold tripped back, arse hit the deck.

The hand dissolved and air came through,
The barbarian laughed, and curses he threw.
He took one step and failed to see,
The spear that almost pierced his knee.

Now Marigold was losing his sense of thrill,
For all he wanted was something to kill.

Give him bones and give him flesh,
He'll crack and tear and hack and thresh.

Up the stairs did Marigold leap,
And found three stones, with secrets to keep
They groaned and creaked, began to rise,
Feet, knees, stomach, teeth, nose, and eyes.

A trio of skags the stones released,
Finally, some life to make deceased.
Marigold hacked and Marigold slew,
But again and again they returned anew.

For skags are creatures hardy of flesh,
Regrowing and returning and attacking afresh.
Our warrior laughed and swung his great blade,
And into Sear's hilt dropped a vial to aid.

A liquid flowed through the grooves she had etched,
Dousing the sword he now held outstretched.
Crack! On the stones he rang Sear's tip,
Flames burst forth! Give her flesh to strip!

Of all three beasts, Marigold made quick work,
He scoured the room for others that lurked.
Satisfied now that the battle was done,
He looked to the steps and started to run.

Floor number four forced our hero to take,
A second look 'round, for it seemed but a fake.
Away with walls, farewell, goodbye,
And hello to grasses and soil and sky.

To his side rode friends that he knew to be dead,

And ahead crashed a monster, flames blew from its head.
On rukhs they ran forth, steel arms held aloft,
Plunging them deep into belly so soft.

And onto the back of the beast they climbed,
Leaving the ground so far, far behind.
Along the tail and up the spine,
Marigold claimed "This cunt will be mine!"

Into its great eye, the warriors went,
Slashing ánd stabbing, the wyrm was soon spent.
Down it soared, straight to the ground,
Its heart beat once more, the last it would sound.

Marigold leapt down, from atop the head,
And in misery found that his friends were all dead.
As he gazed at eyes that were glazed over white,
He soon came to know they died not in this fight.

The spell was broken, he opened his eyes,
To find a strange man measuring leeches for size.
Our warrior had one of them sucking his blood,
Creating the dream he had had, understood?

Now Marigold raged, for he was not to be bound,
Great hands burst forth, the odd man they found.
Like a melon, his head they easily crushed,
And out of floor four, our Marigold rushed.

The next was a space not unlike the dark Pits,
Bodies swung from above, and blood dripped from great
slits.
At the faces he looked, his mind made a list,
And knew them as clansmen he so sorely missed.

Before he could cut a single one down,
A rip, and a tear, and Marigold frowned.
From within dead ribs a tiny hand clawed,
Once again, Marigold reached for his sword.

But around his great arms a tentacle wrapped,
He was dragged to the floor, immobile and trapped.
Between two bodies the barbarian was stretched,
His sword on his back, too far to be fetched.

Marigold pulled and Marigold swore,
And ripped half a body which fell to the floor.
The tentacle, reaching from portals inside,
Thrashed on the stones, twitched once and then died.

Now Marigold free, his foes he could seize,
Wriggling forth from ruined bodies.
Upon him they leapt, tiny and red,
But Marigold's fists made sure they were dead.

Silence then fell across the vile scene,
Blood magic all 'round, but what did that mean?
Cezare was a sorcerer, soon to be dead,
But what great evils went on in his head?

Marigold strode into the next stair,
He turned 'round once more, gave the room a last glare.
Bodies and blood and bones to see,
Put his palm to his face and whispered "Fuck me."

Floor six held a roughskin, toothy and green,
An old foe of Marigold's, when he was a teen.
One-eyed Korag, the roughskin was named,

And upon our Marigold, his misfortune he blamed.

Korag called in his whole family,
To take from our man his ability to see.
An eye for an eye, and a tooth for a tooth,
Marigold was scared, to tell you the truth.

Just seconds before the finger went in,
An imp ran inside, creating a din.
The roughskins panicked, to see this new foe,
And out of their grip our warrior rolled.

Amidst the furore Marigold came,
To stand before Korag, whose eye dulled with shame.
Marigold thrust his own finger forth,
Into Korag's last eye, and burst it with force.

The old green roughskin wailed his due,
Black was his future, no eyes to see through.
This way and that he spun in his mess,
As Marigold swiftly dispatched the rest.

"Just kill me," begged Korag, despair plain to see,
"Do it yourself," Marigold ignored his plea.
The old roughskin wept as Marigold left,
Had work still to do, the worst yet, he guessed.

The seventh was strangely just like the first,
Marigold's mind now leapt to the worst.
An arm and a leg locked the door right ahead,
And the body before him? Most certainly dead.

He tore the way open, looked out over land,
Only from seven floors up. The drop? It was grand.

A push from behind put our warrior in flight,
He clung to the side with all of his might.

The weasel Dahl had planned this whole mess,
And spoke of his glory, to Marigold's stress.
Marigold climbed, up inch by inch,
And of Dahl's trousers he managed to pinch.

Out came the bastard, and into the sky,
But around Marigold's neck did his skinny arms fly.
This way and that, the barbarian shook,
And Dahl's grip released, the arsehole unhooked.

Down the man fell, to his certain doom,
Marigold heaved himself back into the room.
The door disappeared, the body, the trick,
Not far to Cezare now, the sorcerous prick.

The eighth floor held white sheets and a great bed,
And Marigold's wife somehow back from the dead.
The warrior staggered and stumbled with strife,
The reason he fought to avenge her her life.

The woman was perfect in every way,
And Marigold felt his resolve start to sway.
Her knee found its way up into his stones,
He fell to floor amidst grunting and groans.

Cezare stood beside her, sneering his laugh,
Marigold cursed his ridiculous gaffe.
His wife was quite dead, he'd buried her that day,
But seeing her here had him wanting his way.

The wizard winked out, leaving Marigold cold,

Wife slinked back over, to do as she was told.
Marigold took her within his great arms,
But she leapt from his grasp before he could deal harm.

To the ceiling she clung, a human no more,
And dropped back down, into his neck she tore.
Marigold thought that enough was enough,
And decided to show her that rough play was rough.

Onto the end of the great bed he cast her,
Iron tore through, she cried out for her master.
Marigold pushed down until sure she was done,
And though grim was the work, it seemed he had won.

Battle he wanted, and battle he had,
But when this was done, he knew he'd be glad.
Into the stairwell he stalked once more,
Up to Cezare, to the final floor.

The goat-fucking prick stood behind his book,
He watched Marigold enter, and shot him a look.
The warrior's feet became nothing but pain,
And Marigold saw he was trapped once again.

Cezare then revealed his plans in full,
As Marigold was forced to delay his cull.
A portal opened with Marigold's blood,
And into the tower did true dread flood.

The wizard was gone, left the warrior alone,
To deal with his feet, dragging iron through bone.
Freed from his bonds, the barbarian roared,
"You'll soon come to regret me keeping my sword!"

Into the new world Marigold ran,
Taken aback by black skies and red sand.
The wizard he found, on his knees in the dirt,
Before a great demon, their minds in concert.

With Sear in his hand, the barbarian charged,
And into the frame of the devil he barged.
Deep his blade ate, its flames left unquenched,
Spilling black blood and Cezare became drenched.

With a mighty swing Marigold lopped off its head,
And with a crash and a groan the monster fell dead.
He struck the doomed wizard clean in the nose,
Hauled the bastard away, leaving hell with its woes.

Back in the tower Cezare was flung,
Muttering nonsense in unknown tongue.
Marigold staggered, so close to being spent,
Yet inside the wizard dwelt a demon of torment.

Twisting and stretching and splitting his skin,
Cezare rose up, a foul creature of sin.
Marigold had not a moment to waste,
And leapt for its throat, to give Pit-blood a taste.

A dance with the devil took place there that night,
Our warrior fought hard, would not give up the fight.
In went the knives and in went the teeth,
The demon Cezare became naught but a sheath.

Gnashing and gnawing, so deeply he bit,
And sent the fucked creature straight back to the Pit.
The body, it shrank to original form,
Coughing and wheezing, a mess so forlorn.

Marigold stood with his blade overhead,
Struck down at the prick and rendered him dead.
Finally, Marigold's grim work was done,
Gone was the wizard, some poor bastard's son.

"It's not terrible, but it doesn't sound very… professional," Marigold grumbled, leaning back in his chair as he puffed rings of smoke across the candlelit room.

"I beg your pardon?" cried the poet, a trifle pained.

"I'll be laughed out of the palaces with this shite!"

"Palaces? You wanted palaces? This poem's for naught but inns and taverns."

"Oh."

"You wanted more, my friend? Marigold, I've charted your entire life for free. Free. You understand? Writing is my trade. It's what I get paid for, and here you have months of work and I have no coin to show for it, and barely even enough food and drink to see me through the nights. You'll get a story, a tale. Not an epic. Besides, folk'll enjoy this over an ale or two."

"They'll fucking need it."

"I can tear it up." The poet held the papers between forefingers and thumbs.

"No, no… I just… It's great, really, it is, Ingstadt."

"Somehow, Marigold, I don't believe you. You know, you never complained about the rest of it."

Marigold waved a dismissive hand at his friend and grinned. "I probably wasn't listening."

GRIM WORK

,

24911796R00088

Printed in Great Britain
by Amazon